Summer Twilight
CONFIDENTIAL

by Melissa J. Morgan

Grosset & Dunlap

GROSSET & DUNLAP
Published by the Penguin Group
Penguin Group (USA) Inc., 375 Hudson Street, New York, New York 10014, USA
Penguin Group (Canada), 90 Eglinton Avenue East, Suite 700,
Toronto, Ontario M4P 2Y3, Canada
(a division of Pearson Penguin Canada Inc.)
Penguin Books Ltd., 80 Strand, London WC2R 0RL, England
Penguin Group Ireland, 25 St. Stephen's Green, Dublin 2, Ireland
(a division of Penguin Books Ltd.)
Penguin Group (Australia), 250 Camberwell Road, Camberwell, Victoria 3124, Australia
(a division of Pearson Australia Group Pty. Ltd.)
Penguin Books India Pvt. Ltd., 11 Community Centre, Panchsheel Park,
New Delhi—110 017, India
Penguin Group (NZ), 67 Apollo Drive, Rosedale, North Shore 0632, New Zealand
(a division of Pearson New Zealand Ltd.)
Penguin Books (South Africa) (Pty.) Ltd., 24 Sturdee Avenue,
Rosebank, Johannesburg 2196, South Africa

Penguin Books Ltd., Registered Offices:
80 Strand, London WC2R 0RL, England

Text copyright © 2009 by Grosset & Dunlap. All rights reserved. Published by Grosset & Dunlap,
a division of Penguin Young Readers Group, 345 Hudson Street, New York, New York 10014.
GROSSET & DUNLAP is a trademark of Penguin Group (USA) Inc. Printed in the U.S.A.

Library of Congress Control Number: 2008046374

ISBN 978-0-448-44990-6   10 9 8 7 6 5 4 3 2 1

One

Cassie relaxed back onto her elbows as she gazed across the ocean at the hazy horizon. Swishing her feet and burying them into the cool powdery sand, she watched the purples, oranges, and yellows of the sky meld into one of those impossibly gorgeous sunrises that Kona, Hawaii, was famous for.

This time last year, Cassie would have been squeezing into her wet suit right about now, scarfing down a bowl of cereal, and waxing her board in preparation for an all-day training session in the waves. It had been her daily routine for over four years—ever since she'd gone pro as a surfer.

Back then taking a break from surfing had never been an option. Her daily to-do list, if she'd kept one, would have been filled with stuff like: *practice cutbacks, launch airs, win Triple Crown (eventually)*. Not: *go home to Kona, get job as counselor-in-training at summer camp, enjoy sunrise.*

Yet there she was. In her hometown on Big Island. A C.I.T. at Camp Ohana. Enjoying a sunrise. Which was more than she could say for her cousin, Tori.

"Cass, why am I *outsiiiiiide* instead of in my bed?" Tori moaned. "It's too *earrrrrlyyyy* to be *awaaaaaake*." Propped on one elbow, head tilted, she let her silky blond ponytail slightly graze the sand as she pulled the enormous pair of sunglasses off the top of her head and slipped them on over her groggy blue-green eyes.

Tori was fourteen and an Ohana camper, but you'd never know it by looking at her. Maybe it was because she was from L.A., but the girl practically oozed glamour. Take the silver bikini and the platform wedges she had on. Tori seemed more like a model pulled from the pages of *Teen Vogue* than a kid who'd drink bug juice. (Willingly.)

"Am I wrong, or did you explicitly ask to be the first to know if anything happened with Micah?" Cassie asked. She tried to sound casual, but her heart did a tiny flip at the mere mention of his name. And okay, *maybe* she left out the part about her being so excited about last night's events that she hadn't been able to sleep and had been counting the hours until she could drag Tori out of her bunk and spill the news.

Micah was the boys' surfing C.I.T., a fellow resident of Hawaii, a total cutie in that intense, yet hotly scruffy way that caused Cassie to morph from the smart and sporty girl that she was into some hopeless mute with weak knees. Needless to say, the crush began at first sight.

Apparently Micah liked her, too, but getting together had been way complicated. Tons of miscommunications and a nasty ex-girlfriend named Danica who happened to live in Cassie's bunk *and* who had decided to make it her personal mission to get in the way—complicated. For a while it looked to Cassie as if she and Micah just weren't going to happen. But a girl could be wrong, couldn't she?

"I'm telling you, Tor," she said, nearly bursting inside. "You are so gonna die when you hear this."

"Mmmmf."

Cassie rolled her eyes as Tori made the dramatic

effort of flopping over into the sand, pretending to be lifeless. She poked her cousin. "Wake up, dork."

Tori's eyes popped open. She flipped back onto her side and propped her chin in a hand, seeming energized by the prospect of gossip. "Okay, go."

Cassie leaned in a little closer and smiled. "So, remember last night after the dance when you came in the dining hall to show me the coral that guy Lance gave you?"

"Uh-huh," Tori replied with a sly grin. *"And?"*

"Well . . . a few minutes after you left, Micah walked in and asked me to dance!"

"No *way*!" Tori cried, then paused. "But, um, a little late, wasn't he? The Tiki Dance was, like, over? No music?"

"I know," Cassie said. "But then he gave me this shy look and pulled out his iPod and we shared the headphones . . . It was so cute and romantic and we danced and talked and now he knows how much I like him and I know how he feels about me *and* . . . he even gave me this." She extended her tanned right leg so that Tori could observe the pretty anklet that Micah had bought her while in Waikiki—a band of delicate braided leather adorned with a tiny seashell flower. "Even when he was at the intercamp surfing competition he was thinking of me. Can you believe it, Tor? I can't believe it. Can you?"

Clearly she was babbling, so she shut up and waited for her cousin to ask her the obvious question.

"So, did you kiss him?"

"Y-to-the-E-to-the *YES!*" Cassie smiled wide, remembering every detail of the scene: her body tingling when he placed his hands around her waist, breathing in the fresh soapy scent of his skin as they'd danced, how he'd stopped for a moment to look at her before leaning in for a soft, gentle kiss on the lips . . . It was as exciting and momentous as when she'd caught some green in the barrel of her first ten-foot wave. No, maybe better than that.

I knew coming to Ohana would give me time to get my head straight, she thought. *But I never imagined that I'd meet my first real boyfriend here. Bonus!*

"I guess by that goofy look on your face, the kiss was pretty good?" Tori asked.

"Awesome . . . perfect," Cassie said with a sigh.

Tori squinted at Cassie as if she were seeing

something new for the first time. "Cassie? That wasn't, like, your . . . *first* kiss . . . was it?"

"Does kissing Charlie in that truth or dare game we played on the first night of camp count?" Cassie asked. Judging by the eye-roll she got in return, Tori's answer was a clear *no*.

Cassie sat up, feeling a hot blush creep into her cheeks. How could she admit that she'd seen less kissing action than her younger cousin, who was barely a high school freshman? Cassie pulled her feet free from the sand and focused intensely on brushing them off. *Why is she still looking at me? Stop looking at me. What's the big deal?* Finally she couldn't take it any longer. "How many different ways can I say it, Tor? . . . I've never really done anything more than hold hands with a boy! Okay?!"

"Awwww, Cassssssieeeee!" Tori scooted over to give her cousin a hug. "Your first real kiss. How sweeeeeet! And to think, this true love story is all because of *moi*." She held up a hand. "No, no, Cass. Don't worry. No need to thank me."

"Huh?" Cassie asked. "For what?"

Tori rolled her eyes and looked at Cassie as if to say *duh*! "Hel-*lo*? Did Micah not see you in that fabulous gold bathing suit that I gave you for your birthday and fall *instantly* in love? Which, may I remind you, I had to practically *beg* you to try on? Why, Cass? *Why?* It was D&G, for God's sake!"

Cassie cringed at the memory. On the first day of camp, Micah had accidentally barged into the wrong bunk while Cassie was showing Tori her best *America's Next Top Model* imitation in that awful one-piece that barely covered the essentials. "I doubt it was instant," she said, surveying the blue surfing shirt and black boardies that she was now wearing, which were definitely more her style. "And who said anything about love? Right now, we're in *like*. Like, *a lot*. He's supposed to meet me out here in a little while."

"I just wish that Danica had seen it . . ." Tori murmured.

"What? The bathing suit?" Cassie asked. "She probably has."

"No. Not *that*," Tori told her. "I'm talking about the kiss. Maybe if Danica saw it she'd get a clue and finally give it up. Micah is into *you*—not her."

"Somehow, I don't think Danica is into giving up *anything*," Cassie said. "Especially if it has to do with me."

"Well . . . yeah," Tori said plainly. "I mean, think about it: a) her old boyfriend, who I heard she dumped *brutally* last year, has the hots for you, b) you're a way better surfer than she is, and c) you are much, *much* prettier. But the poor girl can't help it if she doesn't have our family's genetics. Life just isn't fair in that way, I guess."

Cassie laughed. Her cousin was too much. Unfortunately, Danica was gorgeous. Granted, it was in that bleachy blond, non-SPF-wearing way, but she was still good-looking—for now.

"Oh, *gawd*. Speak of The Devil Wears Roxy." Reclining back into the sand, Tori motioned vaguely toward the left flank of the camp's beachfront, where the waves were beginning to break nicely.

There she was. Wearing a white bikini top and matching board shorts, Danica dropped her bright pink surfboard flat on the sand and sat down next to it, her long pale blond hair falling neatly around her shoulders as she stared quietly into the sea.

Cassie observed her for a few minutes. Danica wasn't in some kind of meditative state. No, Cassie knew exactly what the girl was up to. She was reading the waves, trying to figure out the pattern of the riptide so she'd know where to find the best ride. It was something Cassie used to do every day. But that was before the *incident*—before she was nearly chewed up by a shark.

Cassie took her focus off Danica for a moment to glance at the shiny new lemon-colored surfboard planted upright in the sand a few feet away. It had been collecting dust in the corner of her bunk since she'd arrived at Camp Ohana, and Cassie wasn't exactly sure why she'd brought it with her this morning. It wasn't as if she really expected to use it after her gossip-fest with Tori.

More like *hoped*.

Why is it so hard to bring my surfboard back into the water? Cassie demanded silently as she watched Danica rise to her feet.

Minutes later, Danica was paddling strongly through the small waves, guiding herself farther out into the deep to where the real surf would form. At the moment, the water lay flat. Danica hoisted herself up to straddle her board, then she stretched her arms above her head and waited, never once taking her eyes off the horizon.

Cassie felt the sudden urge to grab her surfboard

and paddle out to join her. Not because she liked Danica very much—or even *at all*, really—but because one of the parts of surfing that she missed most was just being out there with the other surfers. They'd all lounge on their boards and pass the time until the perfect swell came along. Joking around, talking technique, listening to the inevitable tale of some perfect barrel ride that conveniently had no spectators, Cassie liked the whole camaraderie of it all.

It wasn't long ago that she was waking at the crack of dawn, speed-dialing the surf report, then paddling out just like every other surfer who took the sport seriously. She missed it.

She missed being a surfer.

She missed the connection with the ocean.

She should have been *out* there.

Then just do it, Cassie thought. *Just grab your board and take it out. What's your problem? Do it. Do it!* She glanced at her surfboard again, and took a deep breath. *You can do this, Cass. It's okay. Piece of cake. Come on. In three . . . two . . . one . . .*

But no.

It wasn't okay.

A familiar wave of nausea engulfed her stomach at the thought of being facedown on her board, having her arms and legs dangling in the deep green waters like bait. Her head told her that she was being silly—that the odds of a second shark encounter were pretty small. And it wasn't as if anything *really* happened the first time. So why couldn't she just get over it already?

Because something almost *happened*, she thought with a shiver. *A few more inches and that shark could have taken a bite out of my leg instead of my surfboard.*

Feeling light-headed, Cassie lowered her face between her knees to breathe it out, knowing the whole "moving on" thing was something she still needed to work on. That was why she was a C.I.T. at the camp and not out on the surfing circuit. She was giving herself time to get her nerve back. And she still had weeks until the summer ended. That was plenty of time. Wasn't it?

Cassie searched for Danica again in the sea. A crest was coming in and Cassie saw her paddle hard toward shore to take it. Danica's board caught hold of the wave and she quickly popped up onto her feet and rode it, cutting back to the left, then to the right, then quickly snapping up to catch the lip.

"Whoa," Cassie breathed. She had seen Danica surf well at the water-sports expo at camp a couple of weeks ago, but she had no idea . . . "Tori, did you see that wicked snap?"

Tori didn't answer. Instead, soft rhythmic breathing sounded from her nose. And what was that? Was she snoring a little?

"Tor?" Her cousin's sunglasses made it impossible to confirm if the girl was really sleeping, but Cassie thought it safe to assume that she was. She smiled and shook her head knowingly. Tori was usually quite the perky girl—*after* noon.

As the morning sun rose higher, Cassie watched Danica tear through wave after wave, totally killing it out there.

Oh. My. God. The girl is fearless! As a surfer, Cassie had to respect that—even if Danica was seriously cranky and competitive, like, all the time. And, all right, perhaps there was a *tiny* bit envy involved, too. *I want to be able to ride like that again*, she thought.

Cassie knew she had to get her act in gear if it

was ever going to happen. At least her C.I.T. duties had forced her to go back into the ocean again and she'd gone about waist-deep a few times to teach Tori the basics of surfing, without any major panic attacks. Next thing to do was get back on her surfboard for real. Maybe if she did it slowly, in stages, it wouldn't be so scary.

End of the summer, Cassie reminded herself. *That's my timeline. By the end of summer, I'll be back to my old self again.*

She had to be.

Danica felt her back muscles burn as she paddled for her next ride. She sucked in a deep breath and pushed down on her surfboard as hard as she could, then duck-dived underneath the oncoming wave. Seconds later, she surfaced with the white water crashing behind her.

She powered on, spotting what was sure to be a five-footer coming toward her from the left. Her stomach fluttered in familiar anticipation as she turned and prepared to go for it. Feeling the wave take hold of her board, she drove harder, then leaped to her feet. *Cut right, cut left, cut, cut* . . . Danica's body instinctively gave her the motions in perfect form. She felt a rush as she put Mother Nature in her place. This time.

So why couldn't she do it last week at the surfing competition in Waikiki?

Because the waves were three times bigger in Oahu than on Big Island—and ten times larger than the ones in Florida, where she was from?

No, Danica thought. *No. Excuses.*

She saw her next wave, took it, and tore it to shreds.

See? She *was* a good surfer. A *great* surfer. But it meant nothing if she couldn't perform when it counted. Like, when there were prizes involved and television cameras and important people there who were sure to recognize her obvious talent—if she could just get it together long enough to show it to them.

A few minutes later another wave came crashing toward her. Danica went for it, this time snapping up onto the crest, taking some air, then cutting back and forth until the wave was dead.

No. There was no excuse for letting some random girl psych her out at the competition. And over what? A stupid scratch on her leg? Was that really why Danica bailed within, like, thirty seconds on her first run? Danica usually ruled when it came to intimidation. How could she let some *nobody* talk smack to *her*? And win?

Danica took her next ride, trying to put it behind her, but the memory lingered like a rotten smell. It was bad enough that she'd heard the whispers after the Camp Ohana water-sports expo last week. The ones that said it was Cassie who should have represented in Waikiki, not she.

But the supposed professional surfer didn't feel like getting wet on the day of the expo, Danica remembered. Actually, now that she thought about it, she couldn't recall Cassie getting on her board all summer. What was up with that? Did Cassie think she was too good to surf the small waves?

Whatever. It didn't matter. Danica knew she'd had something to prove in Waikiki, which had added to the pressure. But she shouldn't have messed up like that.

I didn't want it bad enough, she reminded

herself. That's what she'd decided on the way back to camp, anyway. And maybe it was true.

As Danica paddled out for the next wave, her mind drifted from the intercamp competition to Micah. Oahu was supposed to be about more than just proving her surf skills. It was supposed to be where she flirted her way back to her ex-boyfriend.

Who cared if Danica thought Micah was a little blah at times? He was still a hottie, and he was still an okay kisser, and there was still the rest of the summer to consider.

And they had a good time together on their little trip, didn't they? Things had been looking up. They even hung out at the Camp Ohana Tiki Dance last night. So why, then, did Danica witness—horror of horrors—Micah and Cassie kissing *after* the dance?

What? Are they, like, together *now?* The thought of it turned her stomach.

After all, to Danica, Micah was kind of like an old comfy sweater. *Her* sweater. Maybe it didn't fit quite right anymore, but she still *liked* it—sort of—and if she had nothing else to wear, it would totally keep her warm in a cold movie theater.

And Danica was *not* about to give *her* sweater to *Cassie*.

She spotted a swell in the distance and had a feeling that the next wave was going to be awesome—the kind that started the day off right. If she surfed this one in perfectly, she knew it would put her in a better mood.

Danica turned her board toward the shore and paddled slowly at first, then faster as the wave approached. Her heart pounded hard in her chest as she felt the hugeness of the water around her. The moment Danica felt her board's fin take hold of the wave, she popped up onto her feet. Then her stomach dropped as the board free-fell into the curl.

I love that part, she thought, then crossed forward and backward on her board as she rode the wave. Before long she saw a chance to snap up onto the lip. Just as she took it, the sickening image of Micah and Cassie swapping spit in the canteen entered her brain.

Ew.

Only a fraction of a second off, Danica overshot the crest and felt her body propel in the opposite direction of her surfboard. With barely enough time to hold her breath, she crashed sideways into the water and felt herself go under.

Sudden silence.

Her body tossed deeper and deeper.

She couldn't hear herself cry out in pain as her leg brushed hard against a bed of jagged rocks. Knowing not to panic, Danica found the way up and swam for it, finally surfacing to the din of the crashing sea and gasping deeply for air.

She was okay—except that she noticed her leash had snapped and now she had to look for her surfboard. Eager to find it in one piece, Danica swooshed to the left and then to the right as she treaded water. She shaded her eyes from the sun and scanned the surface of the ocean, hoping for a glimpse of hot pink but seeing none.

Maybe it washed to shore, she thought and turned around.

When she found that it had, she almost wished that she hadn't. Because there, ankle-deep in the sea, was Cassie Hamilton fishing Danica's hot-pink board out of the water.

"Great. She saw me get rolled," Danica muttered, not sure why she cared. She took her time swimming back to shore, figuring that Cassie would get tired of waiting and leave her board on the sand to go do whatever it is that she did.

Instead, Cassie propped the board up and just stood there, *staring*, as if she were analyzing Danica's every stroke as she swam back to shore.

It killed Danica to say this, but she knew she had no choice. "Thanks."

"No problem. You all right?" Cassie asked, holding out the board. "Maybe you should get the nurse to look at that." She gestured to Danica's leg.

Danica checked her left thigh, which was kind of scraped up and bleeding a little, but she'd seen worse. "It's fine," she said, taking the board. Now what? Cassie didn't look as if she was going anywhere. "Uh, *thanks*?" she repeated, meaning *time to split now*, but Cassie didn't seem to get the hint.

Instead Cassie said, "You were really great out there. I was watching you."

Wait. A compliment from the pro surfer? That was new. Danica's initial urge to tell Cassie to *stop* stalking her drifted away. "Thanks," she said again.

"You were totally fierce," Cassie went on. "I mean, the way you were attacking those waves like you *owned* them? But when you went for the lip of the last one I was like, 'No! Don't do it!'" She pretended to cover her eyes with her hands.

Why do I feel like I just got sucker punched? Is she actually making fun of me? Danica wondered, getting annoyed. Normally she wouldn't mind a little friendly teasing, but Danica wouldn't exactly call Cassie a friend—not even close. "Oh, were you?" she asked.

"Uh-huh." Cassie nodded. "We weren't sure if you were gonna make it out *alive* after that one."

We? She's rubbing Micah in my face, too? Danica's blood began to boil. She knew Cassie's sugary oh-I-might-be-a-pro-surfer-but-I'm-still-totally-humble act was fake. *Witch.*

"I could give you a few pointers, if you want," Cassie added with a friendly smile. "And hey, I won't even charge you!"

So not funny, Danica thought.

Normally *she* was the one who dished out the snark, not Cassie. The balance of the universe was definitely out of whack. It needed to be fixed.

"Huh," Danica said, steely-eyed. "I find it interesting that *you* want to give *me* pointers.

24

Aren't you the one who's barely put her big toe in the water all summer?" she asked, with a mildly amused expression on her face. "See, unlike you, I'll be getting back on my board the first chance I get. Because, unlike you? I'm not afraid of *fish*."

Maybe it was a little harsh, but hey.

Cassie's smile faded into a thin-lipped line. "I don't know why I even *try* to be nice to you." She said it with such feeling, but considering their history, Danica wasn't buying it. Plus she didn't *need* Cassie to be nice to her.

"So then don't," Danica said with a shrug.

"Fine," Cassie replied. "You know, when I saw you surfing out there I thought we could bury the hatchet and call a truce or something. Whatever. If you're gonna just twist around my words and misinterpret what I say, then we might as well just forget it." She turned in her turquoise flip-flops and marched up the sand toward the palms.

Danica rolled her eyes. She wouldn't have said *anything* if Cassie hadn't insulted her. Besides, Danica had been attending Camp Ohana since the age of nine—she became a C.I.T. this year at sixteen.

She could say whatever she wanted. She'd *earned* her rightful place at the top of the food chain.

She was about to head for the showers when she noticed a tall, tanned guy in a longish orange bathing suit, holding a white T-shirt, jogging down the beach. As the boy came closer, she realized it was Micah.

Isn't he supposed to be hanging with Cassie? Danica wondered, remembering the *"we"* comment. She looked up the beach to find Cassie gently shaking awake her cousin, Tori, who seemed to have fallen asleep on the beach. *Oops. Guess I was wrong.*

And maybe she was wrong about the Micah-and-Cassie status, too, because there he was, headed straight for Danica—*not* Cassie—and looking fine with his lean body flexing at every stride and his dark wavy hair curling around his ears.

"Heyyyy! You're late," she said flashing him a playful smile. "Just missed some hella-good surf. Did you see me out there?" She knew that he hadn't, but it was an opportunity to talk about the awesome waves she caught—minus the last one, of course.

"Sorry, I missed it," Micah said, though he didn't exactly sound as if he meant it.

"Oh." She tried not to notice that he was kind of looking over her shoulder. "No worries. Anyway, let's go to the canteen and grab an early breakfast before the little monsters get there. I'm starved."

"Uh . . . sorry. Can't," he said. "Um, you haven't seen . . . Cassie, have you? I was supposed to meet her out here but I'm a little late."

Ouch.

Feeling numb, Danica nodded in the direction of the palms. She'd regretted breaking up with Micah at the end of camp last summer, but she kind of just assumed that this summer they'd just pick up where they'd left off. At least that had been Danica's plan for camp.

And we would've been hanging out by now if it weren't for her, she thought, watching Micah's brown eyes brighten when he spotted Cassie, who was now helping Tori to her feet.

Why did she have to come here? Danica seethed.

Before Cassie, Danica was the best surfer at camp. She was the queen bee—everybody loved her. She could practically hypnotize a boy with a single glance. But now . . .

27

Without even a "thanks," Micah bolted up the sand to where Cassie and Tori were.

Why does he have to like her? Anyone but her.

Then Danica thought she noticed Cassie glance in her direction before giving Micah a lame peck on the cheek, rubbing it in even more.

So that's how she wants to play this, Danica thought. *Does she really think I'm going to step aside and let her steal my number one spot, without a fight? I don't think so.*

She hoped that Cassie was enjoying the victory—really—because it wouldn't last long. Danica knew she could get Micah back if she really wanted him . . . and that she could be a pro surfer, too—*if* she wanted it.

No, she could do better than that.

She could totally mess a little with Cassie's perfect life.

Just like Cassie messed with hers.

Two

Micah could almost feel Danica's eyes boring holes into the back of his skull as he jogged toward Cassie and kissed her hello.

His heart pulsing, he wasn't sure if bumping into his *old* girlfriend on the way to meeting his *new* girlfriend had him unsettled, or if it was Cassie looking so cute in her little surfer-girl bathing suit that was making him nervous. He liked that she was casual and natural and didn't try to look hot all the time, which, of course, made her even hotter.

Micah was glad that he'd gotten up the nerve to talk to Cassie after the Tiki Dance last night. He'd felt like a jerk for accusing her of liking some dude named Bo. Thing is, as soon as it came out of his mouth, he'd had a feeling that he'd gotten the whole thing wrong.

It could have had something to do with Bo being a pro surfer and Micah being a *wannabe* pro, though Micah was seriously working on changing the wannabe part. Still, being around a major presence like Bo—someone who'd practically surfed the globe—had made him feel so . . . *small.* And there were the doubts. Cassie was beautiful and a talented surfer and probably totally out of his league. Sometimes he wondered why she would even *want* to be with a guy like him.

In the end, Micah found out that Cassie and Bo were only surfing buddies, but by then, the damage had been done. So when he saw Cassie there, alone, sweeping up the dining hall after the dance, he knew that he'd be kicking himself if he didn't at least *try* to make things right.

He apologized. She accepted. And now there they were.

A second chance. Or was it a third?

"Sorry I'm late," he said to Cassie. "One of the guys in my bunk thought it'd be funny to pull the plug to my alarm clock." Lame, but true.

"Don't worry about it," Cassie said casually and without a hint of sarcasm. "Tori and I were here chillin', watching the waves." Her eyes sparkled when she smiled at him.

"Nice," Micah said, thinking how cool it was that Cassie was so laid-back about it. If it were Danica standing there, she'd give him her typical icy glare, followed by an all-day guilt trip, ending with an argument. Not wanting to seem like a complete hound, Micah figured he should probably say something to Cassie's cousin. "'Sup, Tori?"

Tori removed her sunglasses. "Hey."

It was then Micah noticed that the area around Tori's eyes was pale but the regions above and below them were a blotchy bright pink. "Dude, what happened to your *face*?" he asked her.

"Nothing." Tori glanced warily at Cassie, then immediately removed the mini compact she had sticking out the side of her bikini bottoms. She noticed Micah's amusement at the mirror. "What? It's for emergencies. You never know when you're going to have to signal for help or start a fire to boil water or . . ." She opened it and gasped at her reflection. "Oh, no! We came out before sunrise and I totally forgot to apply my SPF!" she cried, inspecting her sunburned face at all angles. "I'm hideous!" She turned to Cassie.

"Why didn't you *tell* me I was burning? You know my skin is supersensitive—like a baby's bottom."

"You mean you have diaper rash on your face?" Micah joked, and Tori cut him a dirty look.

"Sorry, Tor. I didn't notice it, I swear." Cassie took her cousin's chin in her hand. "Let me see."

"Ow!"

"It's not so bad. I'll bet you could, you know, even it out with a little makeup?" Cassie suggested.

"Oh, God. You think?" she said sarcastically, then stomped up the path toward the *pinao* bunk, where she was staying. "Carlie, Tasha! Get me my bronzer, quick!"

Cassie turned to Micah. "I think she's upset."

Do not laugh, Micah thought, watching Tori scurry away in her platform sandals. *Do not laugh at Cassie's cousin. Do . . . not . . .*

On the fifth second he cracked. "Bahahahahahahah!"

"Stop! It's . . . not . . . funny!" Cassie said, but she was giggling now, too.

A few short minutes later, they'd caught their breath and were left with a slightly awkward silence. Normally this would be Micah's cue to lean in and kiss her again—a more meaningful kiss—but he held back.

If it were anyone else he might have just gone for it, right then and there, but this was Cassie. He didn't want to plant one on her just because they didn't know what to talk about. Plus, after all the drama it took for them to finally get together, officially, he wasn't sure if a bold move would freak her out.

In short, he needed a sign.

Preferably something with blinking lights that said *Kiss me!* across her forehead, but he'd settle for a flirty smile. And, hey, if Cassie totally wanted to kiss *him* without warning? Well, he'd be cool with that, too.

Micah's and Cassie's hands instinctively entwined as they headed up the path. A sign? *Cool*, Micah thought, though he wasn't sure where they were going. *Not cool*. He wasn't sure what to say next, either. He tried to will some witty conversation out of his mouth but all he came up with was dead air.

Ask her a question, Micah thought. *Questions are good.*

"So, what did you want to show me?" Cassie said, beating him to it.

Correction. Questions were good . . . except for *that* one.

Last night, as he and Cassie were saying good night, Micah had asked her to meet him in the early morning. When Cassie asked why, he replied with the first thing that came to his mind—that he wanted to show her something. Really, it was an excuse for them to have some alone time before camp activities began and the day got crazy. But saying that out loud seemed too weird. He figured he'd come up with an impressive place to take her, anyway—no problem. *Yeah, right.*

Micah was hoping for a sudden burst of inspiration but all that came out of his mouth was, "Uhhh . . ." *Dude, open trap. Spew words. You've never had trouble talking to Cassie. Why is it so hard now?* "I was thinking of, uh, this . . . *place*." He cringed as it came out. *Good one, Micah.*

"Ooh, mysterious," Cassie said.

Thankfully the C.I.T. director, Simona, emerged from the administrative hut a moment later and put Micah out of his misery. "Cassie Hamilton—just who I was looking for. Phone call for you," she said, waving a cordless receiver.

"Okay. Thanks." Cassie jogged up the steps

to the porch and took the phone. "Hello? Oh, hey, Kiera . . ." she said as Simona disappeared into the building.

Good, Micah thought, leaning on a nearby palm tree. This would give him time to get a clue. And he did. He decided to take her to the tide pools. The pools were quiet. Private. A place to have a real conversation without getting interrupted. Or spied on by ex-girlfriends. Maybe a place to kiss Cassie again, too? Hopefully.

"What? When? Oh. That's great," Cassie was saying.

Micah tried not to stare while she was talking but he noticed that her brows were furrowed and she was massaging her left temple as if she had a headache. Clearly she wasn't too happy with whoever Kiera was.

"Yeah. Me too. See you then, Kiera. Bye." Cassie smiled weakly at Micah, then went inside the building to return the phone.

"Ready to go?" Micah asked when she came out a minute later.

"Sure. Yeah," Cassie replied, but she sounded distracted.

"What's up? Did you get some bad news or something?"

"Not really . . ." Cassie said. "Well, I guess. Maybe," she added, changing her mind. "That was my surfing coach on the phone. She's coming to Big Island for a *little visit* on Monday. Translation? She wants to find out how I've been surfing lately."

"Oh," Micah said. He knew all about Cassie's run-in with a shark a few months earlier. He also knew that she was still super freaked about surfing. He'd found out the hard way—by taking her to this hidden spot with the sweetest waves for their first date, thinking he'd help her get over the fear.

Bad idea. It was almost their last date.

"I've got to get back on track somehow," Cassie went on, almost to herself. "I'm a surfer who doesn't surf." She paused and looked at Micah. "You wouldn't want to . . . help me, would you? You know, whip my butt into shape before Kiera gets here?"

"You want *me* to help you?" Micah's lips curled into a smile. She trusted him that much? That *had* to be a good sign. Right? It was also a lot of pressure. She was a pro surfer, he wasn't. And there was the time factor. "You do realize that we've got a whole two days before your coach gets here."

"You don't have to do it if you don't want to," she added quickly.

"Oh, I *want* to . . ." he said, smiling at the thought of it. "You know . . . this training . . . it's going to require hours of work," he said. "So we're going to be together *a lot.*"

"Uh-huh." Cassie nodded. "We'll probably have to spend, like, every spare minute with each other," she said knowingly. "But I guess I'm willing to suffer for my surfing," she tacked on with a devilish grin.

Cute.

"Oh, yeah?" Micah reached out to tickle Cassie's ribs. "Suffer?"

"No! I'm too ticklish!" Cassie squealed and giggled. She slipped past him with a flirty smile, then bolted like a gecko down the path, back toward the ocean.

Micah laughed and gave chase. He'd do whatever it took to help Cassie get back on her board, no doubt. But he had to do something else first.

He had to kiss her.

"Go, go, go!" Cassie called out to the girls in the fast lane of the pool the next morning. "You guys are strong. Think swimming. That's it. No stopping! That means *you*, Tiffany!"

Breathing hard, Tiffany squinted up at Cassie from the water, her long dark hair slicked to her head with water. "When I said we wanted challenging workouts, I didn't mean *Olympic* workouts," she moaned.

"You can do it, Tiff," Cassie said. "Just think how amazing you'll be by end of the summer. Now, *go*."

Tiffany sighed, dipped her face into the water, and pushed her feet off the wall of the pool.

Cassie blew the whistle around her neck. "Keep it up, girls! Ten more minutes of freestyle and we're done for the day!" She knew she was being a little tough on the A-group, but they could handle it. Watching Tiffany and the other twelve-year-olds zoom gracefully from end to end of the pool was proof alone.

It was also kind of inspiring. In fact, Cassie was beginning to get psyched for her own workout with Micah later. Would today be the day she got back on her board and surfed without fear?

For once Cassie had good vibes about it all—even if a lot was riding on today. Simona had kept the C.I.T.s so busy yesterday that she and Micah had to cancel last evening's training session to do kitchen duty. But after lunch they had the rest of the afternoon to themselves and, if all went well, Cassie would be back to her old surfing self in time for Kiera's little visit.

Cassie blew her whistle and motioned for the girls to exit the pool. "Great job, guys! See you back here tomorrow!" She grabbed her shorts off a nearby chair, pulled them on over her red Camp Ohana bathing suit, and threw her towel over her shoulder.

"Hey, Cassie! Wait up!" Cassie's bunkmate, Andi, called to her from the pool shed, her auburn curls bobbing as she waved. She dropped in a stack of kickboards, closed it up, then power walked on over.

"What's up?" Cassie asked.

"Not much. Thought I'd head over to the mess hall. You going?"

"Uh-huh," Cassie said, picking up her pace to match Andi's. They crossed the pool area and took the path marked by an arrow-shaped sign that read MESS HALL in yellow paint.

Surprisingly, when they approached the office, Andi slowed down to a crawl, then stopped. "Do you think I should ask Charlie if he wants to go to lunch with us?" she asked in a low voice.

"Sure. Why not?"

Andi shrugged. "Well, for one thing, he's barely looked at me since the Tiki Dance. I mean, I thought . . ." She trailed off. "I don't know what I thought."

Cassie couldn't hold back her grin. She knew that Charlie had agonized over asking Andi to dance due to his major crush on her. "You totally like him! That's so cool!"

"Shh!" She looked at the office, then back at Cassie.

Cassie touched Andi's shoulder. "Trust me on this one. Charlie would *love* it if you asked him to come to lunch with us," she said. "Believe me."

"Really?" Andi brightened. "Then I'm going in." She bounded up the stairs two at a time. When she reached the lanai, she turned and whispered, "Wish me luck!"

That was it? Just like that? Cassie crossed her fingers and held them up as Andi disappeared through the doorway, wishing she could be as bold as Andi—or

Tori for that matter—when it came to boys. Seconds later Andi was back outside. Alone. Cassie gave her a questioning look.

"We just missed him. Simona said he went to lunch ten minutes ago." Andi skipped down the stairs and continued along the path without stopping. "Let's hurry. He's probably still in the mess hall."

Cassie followed Andi, her flip-flops crunching on the pebble-strewn walkway. She had to admit that her bunkmate had guts. "You know what I like about you, Andi?" she began. "You always go for it, no matter what *it* is."

"Maybe with sports, yeah. But boys?" Andi shook her head. "I've had a crush on Charlie since *forever*. I kind of have a thing for pasty guys with glasses," she admitted. "But every time I work up the nerve to talk to him, I always chicken out at the last minute. I usually just pretend that I'm on my way somewhere and zoom past him with a quick, *Hey*."

"Charlie mentioned that," Cassie recalled. "He said he couldn't get you to stop long enough to ask you out."

"Oh, God." Andi covered her face with her hands, then swept them through her bouncy auburn curls. "Well, at least now I know he likes me, too. So, I have nothing to worry about. By ze end of lunch he vill beeee minnnne," she added, rubbing her palms together maniacally.

Cassie laughed. "Good luck with that," she said as they entered the canteen.

Andi made a beeline for Charlie, who was by the salad bar in the center of the room, and Cassie picked up a tray and began browsing the sandwiches. She was considering a plate with turkey on wheat and a scrawny pickle slice when she spotted Tori coming over, who, by the way, was sporting a serious Saint-Tropez tan without a hint of sunburn. She seemed to be in a better mood from this morning.

"Looking good," Cassie said, gesturing to Tori's face. "I guess the bronzer worked, huh?"

"No," Tori said, casually grabbing a tray. "But I went to the medical hut for some aloe vera. And do you *know* what I found out?" she asked with a juicy gossip glint in her eyes.

"What?" Cassie replied, interested.

"That the nurse's aid, Stephanie, is a college student. And guess where she works during the school year?" Tori paused for Cassie to fill in the blank.

Cassie shrugged.

"Sephorrrrra." Tori whispered it with such reverence you might have thought she was speaking about the eighth wonder of the world, not a trendy cosmetics shop. "Stephanie set me up with a free eyeliner. Isn't that sweet?"

"Cool," Cassie said, though admittedly, she didn't bother much with makeup—just a little lip gloss and maybe some mascara, too, if it was a special occasion.

"I *know*," Tori added. "Oh, and she gave me the aloe *and* she let me use some of her fabulous tinted moisturizer that blended with the natural oils of my skin to give me this stunning glow," she said, circling her face with an index finger. "We are *so* lucky to have—Oh my God! He's *here*," she uttered suddenly. *"Don't. Look."*

"At who? Lance the surfer?" Cassie asked. He was Tori's current crush. "Eddie?" He was Tori's on-again, off-again crush.

"Neither," Tori whispered. "It's *Sam*." She plastered a smile on her face and peeked slightly over her shoulder. "I think he might be looking at me. Is he?"

43

Cassie was confused. "Who's *Sam*?"

"We met this morning in the nurse's office. He stepped on a sea urchin and was waiting to get the needles pulled out," she explained. "He was *so* brave—and he's got the most amazing crystal blue eyes . . . oh, and a really cute bandage on his left foot."

"You met a hot boy in the medical hut? Amazing," Cassie said, shaking her head. "What did you do? Pay a witch doctor to make you a special boy-attracting perfume?"

"Nah. This wrinkly sha-woman who lives in the back room of a tattoo parlor in West Hollywood taught me the art of flirting for only three payments of $19.95," Tori cracked. "Thank *God* for infomercials . . . So, is he looking at me?"

Cassie did the casual I'm-just-gonna-gaze-at-no-one-in-particular pass with her eyes, scanning the mess hall. Sure enough, she spotted a cute boy, about fourteen, with black hair, blue eyes, and a bandaged foot sitting at a nearby picnic table with two other guys his age. Unfortunately . . . "He's not looking right now."

"Oh." Tori pouted for a second, then said, "He will when we do the walk-by. Come on."

The girls got their food and drinks and weaved through the crowded mess hall, pretending to look for seats. Just as they were *accidentally* passing by Sam's table, Cassie noticed Sam notice Tori.

"Hey," he said, "how's the sunburn?"

"Oh, heyyy." Tori turned, raising her eyebrows as if she were actually surprised. "It's okay, I guess. I see you're doing better, too." She glanced at his bandaged foot. "So. Can I sign your, um, gauze?"

"Sure. But I don't have a pen," he said.

"'Kay." At that moment Tori whipped out her new felt-tip Sephora eyeliner from her shorts pocket and signed her name across the entire top foot, complete with a tiny heart dotting the *i*. "So he doesn't forget me," she whispered to Cassie. "Later, Sam!" She wiggled her fingers at him and then moved on.

"You know you could have your own infomercial, right?" Cassie told Tori once they were out of earshot.

Tori shrugged. "Maybe."

They crossed the mess hall to the corner where the counselors and the C.I.T.s usually sat, only to find Andi barely nibbling on her tuna-fish salad at a table by herself.

"What happened to Charlie?" Cassie asked, sitting across from her.

"You tell me," Andi said. "I was on my way to the salad bar to talk to him, and he practically ran away from me. It was so weird. I know he saw me. Maybe he doesn't like me as much as you think he does."

"No, he totally does," Cassie said, putting it in her mind that she'd ask Charlie what the deal was later.

"I second that," Tori added, then glanced over her shoulder at Sam.

"Anyway. I refuse to be grumpy about it. All this negative energy is giving me zits. See?" Andi pointed out the one itsy-bitsy blemish on her left cheekbone. "Next subject. You and Micah seem pretty cozy lately."

"Maybe," Cassie said, blushing. "We're kind of together now." *Is he really my boyfriend?* She resisted the urge to jump atop the picnic table to do her happy dance, choosing instead to play it cool. She was just about to launch into the story about the Tiki Dance when she spotted Danica and her two cronies, Sasha and Sierra, heading toward their table.

"They are *not* coming over here," Tori murmured under her breath to Cassie.

"Hey, Danica! Sasha! Sierra!" Andi said, waving them over. That was the thing about Andi. She was kind of like the Switzerland of the *nai'a* bunk. She got along with everybody and didn't like to choose sides.

Cassie felt her body tense as Danica, Sasha, and Sierra plunked down their trays.

"Hey, Andi," Danica said, choosing the seat directly opposite Cassie.

Cassie figured Danica was being all weird and primal, somehow trying to mark territory or whatever. But then Danica did something even weirder. She smiled sweetly. At Cassie. With actual teeth and everything. Then she spoke. "Hi."

Cassie raised her chin slightly at Danica, then focused on poking at the turkey sandwich before her. Danica had barely uttered two words to her since yesterday. Something was up, Cassie knew that much, but she didn't know what.

"So . . . um . . . can we talk for a minute?" Danica asked Cassie. "In private? Do you mind?"

Yes, Cassie minded. But she was also curious.

Why was Danica being so nice all of a sudden? What could she have to say?

"I guess so," Cassie said, sliding off the picnic bench. "Be right back," she told the others, then followed Danica outside.

When they rounded the back of the mess hall, Danica turned to Cassie and pursed her lips. Not quite as friendly as the smile a few seconds ago, but not unfriendly, either. "Look," she said. "I've been considering what you said."

Cassie racked her brain, trying to figure out what she could have possibly said that Danica would have given a second thought. *Nada*.

Danica must have noticed this and let out an irritated sigh. "You know. About the *truce*?"

"Oh. Right," Cassie said. "What about it?"

"Well . . . maybe you're right," Danica said. "Maybe we should, you know, be civil or whatever. I mean, what's the point of all this drama, anyway?"

Cassie wanted to mention that Danica was the one who'd started all the drama in the first place, but she held her tongue.

"Anyway, I know I haven't been the easiest person to be around," Danica went on, "and for that . . ." She placed her hand on Cassie's arm. "Well, for that I am truly sorry."

Cassie surveyed Danica's face. It seemed open, honest. Like she really did mean what she was saying. And the words, they were all so perfect. Maybe *too* perfect.

Where was the mean and evil Danica? Cassie wondered. This nice one was kind of creeping her out. "I'm just . . . I'm really surprised," she began. "After yesterday, I mean, I was only trying to help—"

"Yeah. I know," Danica cut her off. "That fish comment I made was way out of line. I mean, *of course* you'd be a little hesitant about getting back into the water after what happened. *Anybody* would. I was just mad at myself for wiping out. But I shouldn't have taken it out on you. I'm sorry."

Cassie found herself softening a little. "Thanks, Danica. For saying that."

"So, do you think we can start over?" Danica asked. "I really am a cool person when I want to be and, believe me, I do. What do you say?"

Cassie wasn't sure. Could she trust the new Danica? Did this girl really want a do-over on their friendship? Or was Cassie somehow being *Punk'd*?

She glanced around, almost expecting to see Sasha and Sierra hiding in the bushes with a video camera. But they weren't, of course.

Maybe I should just give Danica the benefit of the doubt, Cassie decided. *Why not? My life's been full of do-overs lately. One more couldn't hurt. Could it?*

About an hour later, Cassie was lying back on her surfboard, enjoying the sun and holding hands with Micah.

He'd surprised her at the lunch table earlier by taking her hand and telling her to grab her surf gear and to meet him by the Jeep. Thinking that Cassie wouldn't want to surf with an audience, Micah had scored Simona's permission to drive her to that secluded spot he'd taken her to weeks earlier. The one with all the sweet waves.

Cassie brushed aside that it was the same spot where they'd had their first argument, which had been about her not wanting to surf. It seemed so long ago, so irrelevant considering how much everything seemed to have changed since then.

All Cassie knew was that her boyfriend was awesome.

Her boyfriend.

It was still hard to believe.

It was also hard to believe that she was now sort of friends with Danica. Lunch had gone well after their little chat. Cassie had had no idea how much Sasha and Sierra could really talk, since they'd barely spoken to her before said chat. And they could go on about everything: guys, girls, clothes, makeup, and even surfing.

Cassie had felt comfortable enough to mention that her coach was coming to visit her tomorrow and that she wasn't quite ready for it surfwise. Danica was nice to offer to surf with Cassie today, to prepare, but that was when Micah came into the picture.

"You ready?" Micah asked once they were on the beach, sitting up on his aqua short board, his feet straddling it in the sand.

"Ummm . . ." Cassie *wanted* to say yes. She *wanted* to leap to her feet, to shout a flirty, "Race ya!" and charge toward the ocean. But she couldn't. "I think someone put poi on my butt. I'm kind of stuck," she said instead. "But I guess anything's better than eating the stuff." The pasty bland staple in most Hawaiian diets was made from taro roots and was, in a word, gross.

Micah rose to his feet, offered her a hand, and helped her up. "Step one," he said. Then he wrapped her arms around her and pulled her into an embrace. "Step two."

Cassie rested her head on his chest and hugged him back so tightly that she could hear his heart thudding inside.

"You can do this, Cass," he whispered into her hair. "I *know* you can."

Cassie pulled away, nodding, appreciating the pep talk. "I know. Okay," she told him. She had to push past the fear somehow. Micah said she could do it. Kiera had said the same thing, too. Maybe she should take a leap of faith and believe them. "Let's do this."

"That's what I'm talking about." Micah quickly went for his board, and within seconds the cool ocean was lapping at their ankles.

Step three. So far, so good, Cassie thought, wading out to her thighs and then dropping her surfboard into the foamy water. She flopped onto it, arched her back, and began to paddle, surprised by how easy it was.

Then again, Cassie hadn't reached the wall yet.

The wall was an imaginary line that had developed in the ocean shortly after her shark incident. Between the wall and the shore—preferably *on* the shore—Cassie felt okay. Maybe a little nervous, but she could deal.

Once Cassie swam beyond the wall, however, . . . not so much. Her lungs would tighten and her heart would rush and she'd almost always feel as if she were about to lose her lunch—even if she had no lunch to lose. And she'd feel this illogical, uncontrollable, crazy kind of panic well up inside of her—where the only thing she could do was whimper and cry as she raced back to the comfort of the sand.

The worst part was that Cassie never knew where or when the wall would emerge. One minute, she might be fine ten or twenty yards out and the next she might be in major panic mode. The last thing Cassie wanted to be was the camp freak show, which was why she never ventured too far away from the Ohana shoreline.

Cassie turned her head, trying to gauge how

far they were from shore. Just as she did, a rogue wave slapped over her head. "Pppffft!" She spit out a mouthful of water.

"Oh, man. You got *nailed*," Micah said just as a wave hit him straight on in the face. "Ugh. *I* got nailed," he said, laughing. He stopped paddling. "Think this a good spot to catch our first run?"

"Uh-huh," Cassie said, beginning to feel a suspicious tightening in her chest. She was glad that they weren't going any farther.

Micah flipped up, then sat facing Cassie with his legs dangling over one side of his board. Cassie did the same, facing Micah.

"I love it out here," he said as the water slightly rocked their boards. "So quiet."

"Mmm." Cassie used to enjoy the gentle swaying. The ocean's lullaby, she'd called it once. But now, it was kind of making her queasy.

Micah took her hand in his. "Cass? You okay? You look a little pale."

"Mmm," she said again, wondering if there was any way to *discreetly* blow chunks off the side of her board and still look cute.

Uh, that'd be no.

Do not *barf,* Cassie ordered herself. *Do not* . . . She tried to focus on a tiny piece of seaweed stuck to the top of her board when suddenly something nipped her foot!

"Ahhhh!" She pulled her leg up out of the water—too fast—and fell off the other side of her surfboard. She quickly scrambled back atop it. "Something . . . something tried to bite me," she sputtered out, scanning the sea.

Micah was laughing until he saw the panic in her face. "No, Cass. That was me," he said. "I brushed your foot, um, by accident."

"Oh." Cassie felt a flush of embarrassment rush to her cheeks. "*Some*body feels a little stupid right now," she murmured. "I mean, even if it had been a little fish, so what? One time, a crab almost pinched off my big toe, and I didn't care. I kept surfing."

"Oh, yeah? I got that one beat," Micah said. "Once, while I was surfing out in Hilo, I got stung by this monster jellyfish. Seriously painful. I almost broke down and peed on myself because I heard it numbs the hurt."

"Ouch . . . and ew!" Cassie winced. "But that still doesn't come close to—" She froze midsentence.

"What?" Micah asked.

"Um, never mind," Cassie said. "I guess I forgot." Only, she didn't. She was about to say that it didn't come close to being attacked by a shark, and by the sympathetic look on Micah's face, she knew he knew it.

Cassie hadn't meant to go there. Now that she was there, though, she couldn't help wondering what might be lurking beneath them. Her heart pumped harder as she slipped her legs out of the sea and hugged her knees tightly to her chest, suddenly aware of how far away from the shore they were.

If I'm weirded out by a little underwater footsie, maybe coming out here wasn't such a good idea. Maybe I'm not ready. Maybe I should call Kiera and try to—

"Hey, I think that one's got your name on it, Cassie!" Micah said, shielding his eyes from the sun and pointing to the wave forming in the distance. "Get ready to do your thing."

Cassie locked her eyes onto the rising swell, which she gathered would probably turn into a modest three-footer. She could either wimp out like she wanted to or push through the fear. Now that she was staring it in the face, she knew she owed it to Micah and to Kiera to at least try. Maybe to herself, too.

Cassie swallowed hard and turned her surfboard, determined to ride it in. She heard the ocean's roar, felt her board's fin hook into the barreling wave. Now was the time to pop up onto her feet. Why couldn't she get her legs to work?

Her head swirling, Cassie made it to her knees when millions of tiny white spots began flashing before her eyes. She dropped flat again, her lungs pinched tight as she clung to the board, dizzy and too afraid to call for help.

Before she knew it the ocean was tossing her under.

Cassie scraped her way to the surface, only to be pummeled by another wave and knocked back under. Then she felt hands. Micah's hands. They were around her waist and pushing her up onto her surfboard. A moment later he, too, was on the board—behind her, holding her, making sure she didn't fall as he rode them both to shore.

Once out of the water, Cassie dropped to the sand. Humiliated, she felt the sting of tears, but she

57

willed herself not to cry. "Your board. You should find it," she managed to say.

"Later." Micah kneeled beside her. "I'm sorry, Cass. I didn't realize the wave was too much. I never would have made you—"

"It wasn't the wave. It was *me*," she admitted. "I'm scared. *Terrified*. I . . . what is *wrong* with me?" The tears finally capped and slipped down her cheeks. "What if I never get my nerve back?" It was the first time Cassie had allowed herself to say it—to even *think* it, really.

"Hey, hey . . ." Micah swiped gently at her tears then pulled her into his arms. "You will," he said. "I'll help you. You're my girl, right?"

"I am?" Cassie asked, sniffling, but knowing it was true. It seemed like the only spark of goodness to come out of this whole thing.

Micah nodded slightly, his face growing serious as he leaned in to kiss her.

Cassie closed her eyes and wrapped her arms around her boyfriend's neck. No more surfboards, or sharks, or disappointed coaches, or pressure. As their lips touched, it all seemed to melt away. And for one tender moment she forgot to be afraid.

Three

"You can run, but you can't hide!" Micah said the next morning in the Ohana parking lot. His hair dripping wet, he was holding a large bucket of sudsy water on his shoulder. He was supposed to be using the water to clean the camp Jeep in exchange for using it yesterday.

Cassie peeked out from behind the rear bumper of the car. She gripped the nozzle of the hose she was holding, aimed it at Micah, and squeezed. "Gotcha!" she cried, soaking him from head to toe.

"Oh, you are so dead!" Micah laughed and rushed the back of the Jeep.

Cassie tried to make a break for it, but she wasn't fast enough and she squealed as Micah dumped the entire contents of the bucket over her head. "Noooo!" she shouted and giggled as they play-wrestled for the hose. She squeezed the nozzle again, but this time the stream hit the Jeep's tire.

"It's about time you kids got some water *on* the car," Simona said on her way over.

Cassie looked up and her face dropped, not because she and Micah were caught fooling around instead of working, but because Cassie's coach was about two paces behind the C.I.T. director. With her tall muscular frame and short brown bob, Kiera was kind of hard to miss.

"Heyyy! Hiiii!" Cassie tried to sound peppy and happy to see Kiera, as opposed to not-so-secretly dreading the reunion ever since yesterday's surfing debacle. "Aren't you a little early?" *Oops. Slipped out.*

"About ten minutes, maybe," Kiera said with a knowing glint in her eye. "Who's this?" She nodded toward Micah, who had just taken off his sopping shirt and was wringing it out onto the pavement.

Cassie tried really, really hard not to get lost in his rock-solid abs or how his cute green-and-white swim trunks hung loosely on his hips. How could someone so sweet be such a hottie? "Oh, um, him? That's my friend."

"Riiiight," Kiera said. "I figured that. Nice to meet you, Cassie's friend," she called to Micah.

"Huh? Oh." Cassie suddenly got it. "Kiera, Micah. Micah, Kiera," she said, introducing them.

"Hi." Micah gave a friendly wave, and Kiera smiled.

"So. I thought we'd do a little workout. You in?" Kiera asked Cassie.

No. "Sure! Um, just as soon as I finish washing the Jeep," she told her. "That should take, ahhhh . . ." *A half hour? All day?* she thought hopefully.

"Don't worry about the Jeep," Simona broke in. "Micah will finish it up."

"Yeah." Micah nodded. "Go do your thing."

"Thanks!" *For nothing*, Cassie thought. "All righty then." She turned to Kiera. "Let's go get my surfing stuff."

Kiera pulled her own gear from the back of her truck, then followed Cassie down a path to the *nai'a* bunk. Once inside, Cassie crossed to her bed and grabbed her yellow surfboard, which was leaning against the wall by the window.

"Nice board. Love the color," Kiera said, admiring it. "That one's pretty sweet, too," she added, gesturing to the pink board laying flat on Danica's bed as if it were waiting to be waxed.

"That's my roommate's," Cassie told her.

"Cool. A surf buddy. She any good?" Kiera asked.

"I guess so," Cassie replied, though she wasn't sure why the question bugged her. Why was Kiera asking about *Danica*? Shouldn't she be focused on Cassie?

Once on the beach, though, Cassie was soon wishing her coach would focus on anyone *but* her. Like, when Kiera wanted Cassie to dive right in and warm up, but Cassie stalled, saying that she was tight and needed to stretch first.

Then when she'd finished stretching and was ankle-deep in the water with her stomach twisting into a knot, Kiera was right beside her saying, "Surf looks awesome. Come on, let's hit it."

Cassie was relieved when she spotted Tori racing up to them, arms flailing, trying to get her attention. "Quick. Lance is over there and I need a translation. What the heck is a double spinner? And how hard is it, 'cause I told him I can do it?"

Cassie took her time explaining that a double

spinner is when you do two 360-degree body spins on a board and it's pretty easy to do . . . if you happened to have been born on a surfboard, which Tori hadn't been, so she'd better not try it.

"Okay. What about a cheater five?" Tori asked.

Kiera was good-natured about the interruption. But when Cassie was about thigh-deep in the water, feeling dizzy with fear, she clutched her lower belly and turned to her coach. "You know, I have some serious crampage going on," she lied. "Maybe we could do this another day, huh?"

"Right. I don't think so." Kiera planted her hands on her hips. "So, are you going to tell me what's going on, or what?"

Cassie took a deep breath. She could put off surfing, but she couldn't put off coming clean. "It's just . . . maybe I don't feel ready to jump in and pretend like nothing happened." She looked at her coach sheepishly. "Don't be mad, okay?"

"I'm not mad," Kiera said, shaking her head. "I'm worried. This . . . it's so not like you. You used to live to surf. You were fearless. But now . . ." She paused. "Are you sure your new *friend* doesn't have something to do with this? Maybe you're more

63

interested in romantic walks along the beach than training?"

"No!" Cassie said, annoyed that Kiera would even suggest that, though there *had* been a romantic stroll or two. "I'll get it together, Kiera. I swear," she assured her. It came out sounding more certain than she felt. "So you don't have to worry about me."

"It's not only that," Kiera began. She motioned for them to get out of the water. "We need to talk."

Uh-oh. Cassie gulped as she sloshed out of the water behind her coach. Kiera was patient, but she wasn't one of those best-friend types. Her brand of coaching was tough and totally serious. Cassie had a feeling that whatever Kiera had to say, it wouldn't involve much coddling.

Kiera planted her board, grabbed a towel from her duffel on the sand, and tossed it in Cassie's direction. "Sit," she said, and Cassie complied. "I wasn't about to mention this today, but I think it's important for you to know what's going on." She sat next to Cassie, then glanced upward as if searching for a way to begin. When she seemed to choose the right words she said, "I've been receiving a little . . . *pressure* from the Coco Beach people. They're getting anxious, and you don't need me to tell you that's not a good thing."

Coco Beach was a company that made surf wear, boards, and accessories. They were Cassie's main sponsor, which meant they provided all of her gear, paid for her travel and accommodations for surfing events, and gave her a small salary.

In return Coco Beach expected her be the brand's spokesperson, to be *the* role model for young female surfers, and to place top-five in all of her events. *Hey, no pressure. Really.*

"So, what did the Coco Beach people say?" Cassie wanted to know.

"Well . . . that they understand what you're going through, but they feel as if they're missing out on a huge opportunity for publicity," Kiera explained. "You know, the whole 'surfer comes back after shark attack' thing? In a Coco Beach bikini, of course."

"*That's* being *understanding*?" Cassie dried off her legs and threw the towel back into Kiera's bag.

"I know. It's not," Kiera agreed. "But you're a professional, Cassie. At this level, surfing is a business. Competing around the world is expensive. You need money to pay for it. But a sponsor won't help you unless there's something in it for them. You know what I'm talking about, right?"

"Yeah. Exposure." Cassie heaved a sigh. "I need to be seen competing in Coco Beach swimwear, surfing on Coco Beach boards, wearing Coco Beach sunglasses, blah, blah, blah . . ."

"Look. The good news is, Coco Beach's public relations team has convinced *Surf Girl* magazine to do a feature on you," Kiera went on.

"And the bad news?" Cassie asked.

"Truthfully?" Kiera said, and Cassie nodded. "Word is, they're losing confidence, Cassie. They're not a hundred percent sure you're coming back to surfing."

"But it's only been a few months!" Cassie said. "I was totally traumatized. Can't they cut me some slack?"

"I guess they think they are," Kiera replied, "but they also want to see a strong presence in Brazil. The qualifiers are just around the corner. Luckily they're in Honoli'i this year. Do you think you'll be up for it?"

"Yes . . . *definitely*." Maybe if she said it with enough conviction, it would somehow become the truth, Cassie figured.

"Well, maybe you should come back with me to Oahu tomorrow for some intense training just to make sure," Kiera suggested. "What do think?"

I think I'm busted, Cassie thought.

"Umm . . . I don't know. Maybe," she replied. But the reality was, Cassie had no clue how she was supposed to qualify for Brazil even with intense training. *Master barrels when I can't handle basic surfing 101? Is it even possible?*

She watched the tide barely touch her toes, then recede back into the ocean over and over as she tried to process this added layer of information. Should Cassie really pick up and go, ditching her responsibilities at Camp Ohana, when she couldn't say for sure she'd even make it to Brazil? Plus, she and Micah were finally getting close. How could she just leave him?

Cassie was about to ask Kiera how bad it would be if she, say, skipped Brazil this year to focus on placing in Japan, which, no offense to the Brazilians, was a way more important event.

Who knew if Cassie would be up and surfing by then? At the very least it would buy her some extra time. But when she turned to pose the query, Kiera was staring at another surfer in the ocean—at a girl riding a hot pink board—at Danica, who happened to be killing it out there in the waves. Again.

Cassie knew she and Danica were starting to be friends now but, at that moment, Cassie couldn't help not liking her a little. And maybe even a bit more when Kiera said, "Who is that? She's *really* good. Just needs a little work on her bottom turns, but that's nothing that can't be fixed," almost as if she were scouting out new talent.

She wasn't . . . was she?

"I told you. That's my roommate. Or didn't you notice the obnoxious pink surfboard?" Cassie knew it sounded snotty, but who could blame her? Why was *her* coach drooling over Danica's surfing skills? Shouldn't she have been helping Cassie salvage her career? The one they'd both been building together for the last four years? To make matters worse, Danica looked exhilarated and strong as she waded out of the frothy water, carrying her surfboard overhead. She spotted Cassie and Kiera by the water's edge and waved as she crossed the sand in their direction.

"The water is so awesome," she said when she

reached them. "*Tell* me you guys aren't going to sit on the beach all day, 'cause that would be just . . . *wrong*." She planted her board in the sand and smiled brightly at Kiera. "I'm Danica, by the way."

"I'm Kiera Tate, Cassie's surf coach," she said, standing to greet her.

"Oh, really? I had no idea," Danica said with an awkward giggle. "Wow. You're, like, a total legend. Didn't they make a movie about your life or something?"

"Not exactly. It was more about my surfing. I was at the top of the sport, back in the day."

"Oh my God. Everybody knows *that*," Danica gushed. "Right, Cassie?"

Cassie held back her eye roll. Danica was laying it on a little thick. "Yup," she lied.

The truth was, when Kiera had first discovered Cassie only a few miles north up the Kalui Kona beaches of Big Island, Cassie had no clue that her would-be coach had won the infamous Triple Crown. Then again, Cassie had been only twelve years old and not very serious about surfing. Up until then she'd been riding waves for the pure fun of it.

Who knew my hobby would turn into my life?

Or maybe it's not my life anymore. Cassie shook off the thought.

"So I was watching you surf," Kiera was saying. "You have nice lines, Danica. Who's your coach? Maybe I know her."

"A coach?" Danica said, touching a hand to her chest. "No, no. I don't have one. I'm just an amateur. But I am *so* honored you think I'm good enough to have a coach. Wow."

Danica's lovefest was beyond sickening. *And since when does she admit to being an amateur at anything—especially surfing?* Cassie wondered. "Gee, Danica. That's the first time I've heard you say—" she began, but was cut off.

"Let me give you my contact info." Kiera spoke over Cassie as if she wasn't even there. She quickly rooted through her duffel on the sand, then looked up and shrugged. "Oh, I guess I'm all out of business cards at the moment, but Cassie can give you my number. If you ever consider going pro, maybe I can help you out—hook you up with a coach." She exchanged a glance with Cassie. "Not me, of course. I kind of have my hands full right now."

Cassie stared at Kiera. *What's that supposed*

to mean? *Is she planning to "empty" her hands later . . . if I don't make it to Brazil?* Her body trembled as she listened to Kiera then explain how Danica could strengthen her bottom turn. Maybe Kiera really *was* lining up someone new to train. *But, would she do it right in front of me?*

Cassie wasn't sure whether to be upset or angry. It was one thing for a surfer to be dropped by her sponsor, but by her coach?

One of the greatest women in surfing thinks I'm talented. Danica smiled to herself as she strode up the beach with her surfboard under her arm. She knew all she had to do was rock it when it counted. Finally, she made it happen.

She slowed her pace when she overheard Kiera's voice. "Just think about coming home with me tomorrow to train for the qualifying rounds. Okay, Cassie? The summer is almost over and you need to seriously focus if you're going to make it to Brazil."

"I'll think about it," Cassie told her.

A qualifying round? Brazil? What's there to

think about? Danica wondered. If Kiera had asked *her* to train, she'd be racing back to the bunk to pack her bags. Camp Ohana was nice, but, hel-*lo*, it was no *Brazil!*

What a waste. As far as Danica was concerned, Little Miss Pro Surfer Girl was clinically insane. And selfish. And had absolutely no idea how good she had it.

I guess she'll figure it out when I take it all away from her, Danica thought. *If not, she's a bigger loser than I thought she was.*

She took the path back toward her bunk and smiled to herself again. Operation: Destroy Cassie seemed to be working out nicely.

First there was the whole "truce" thing with Cassie. Danica had known it was a long shot—she'd suggested it only to knock Cassie off guard—and Cassie had totally fallen for it. The bonus had come when Kiera showed up out of the blue and offered to help Danica with her surfing and also with finding a coach. Who, quite possibly, was Cassie's soon-to-be ex-coach.

Why not? Didn't Cassie steal Danica's soon-to-be *ex*-ex-boyfriend, Micah? Or he would be—as soon as Danica worked on him a little. She couldn't just let *Cassie* have him, could she? And lucky for Danica, Micah and his bunkmate Ben were ambling down the path in her direction.

God, this was almost *too* easy.

"*There* she is," Ben said. "I've been looking for you all over camp, Danica."

He was cute. Confident. The type of boy Danica usually went for. The thing with Ben was that he knew just how good-looking he was. He *expected* girls to fall all over him—and most did—so maybe he needed to be knocked down a peg.

"And it never occurred to you that I was trying to avoid you?" Danica said. But when Ben grinned again, she realized he thought she was flirting with him. She rolled her eyes and turned to Micah. "So the waves are awesome today. I'd be down with going in again if you wanted to."

"The surfing C.I.T.s want to surf in their spare time, too? Is that all you guys do?" Ben asked. "How about some kneeboarding? A little beach volleyball? Parasailing?"

"Sorry. I like surfing," she told Ben.

Ben turned to Micah for help.

73

"Dude." Micah shrugged. "What can I say? The girl has good taste."

Ben looked upward and shook his head. "They're obsessed," he commented to no one in particular, and backed down the path. "I'll be giving the ten-year-olds their kayak lessons if you need me."

"We won't," Danica chimed in.

"Of course not. You're obsessed with surfing." Ben's brown eyes sparkled at her. "See you guys at the campfire tonight."

"Whatever," Danica said.

"Later," Micah added. Once Ben was gone, he glanced sideways at Danica. "You're not . . . into *him*, are you?"

"Ew. No. Did you not notice that I wasn't exactly friendly?"

"Yeah. Except, that's how you were with me when we first met," Micah reminded her. "On second thought, that's how you are with everyone."

"Shut up." Danica rolled her eyes again, but then something came to her. "Jealous much?"

"Give me a break," Micah said, but he kept shifting his weight and he seemed unable to look her in the eye.

He is *jealous!* Which was a surprise. Or perhaps it wasn't such a surprise. But it was definitely interesting. And maybe it meant Danica should make a move.

"All of the surfing lessons are finished, so Haydee and Zeke don't need us." She smiled devilishly. "Come on. Let's hit the waves. For old times' sake. You in?"

"Totally," he replied. "I'll see what Cassie's up to. Maybe she'll want to go."

Cassie? Nobody invited Cassie. Danica swallowed some nasty commentary and said, "Oh, I think she's kind of busy with her coach. Did you know Kiera Tate was here? As a matter of fact, Kiera saw me surf *and* she thinks I'm good! She offered to help me if I ever want to go pro. She even gave me a few pointers," she added, knowing he'd appreciate how momentous this was for her. "I'm so stoked."

"Cool," Micah said. "So . . . I guess Cassie was surfing, too. You saw her, right?"

"*No*," Danica said, drawing out the word. So much for re-bonding over a common interest. Time to switch up her game. "You know, I'm starting to think *you're* obsessed with something, but it's not surfing." She scoffed. "God, Micah. You used to be so much fun."

"Hey. I'm still fun," Micah said defensively.

Danica blinked.

"I *am*!" Micah declared.

"Okay. You're fun." Danica began down the path toward the bunks again. "See you later, Fun Boy. I mean, *if* you get permission from your girlfriend." She glanced back, expecting to find him right behind her, but instead he was walking in the opposite direction toward the beach. *No! You're supposed to follow me, dummy!*

Danica had only one option left. She had no choice. "Ow!" she cried, pretending to twist her foot in a rut. She dropped her board and clutched her ankle. "Owwwww!"

As anticipated, the Good Samaritan was at her side in a matter of seconds. "Danica! What happened?"

"Twisted my ankle," she said, wincing.

"I'll take you to the nurse, then get Simona."

"No!" Danica cried—a little too loudly. "Um, I mean. It's not that bad. But maybe you could just . . . help me limp back to my bunk?"

"Sure." Micah picked up her board, Danica leaned on him, and they shuffled down the path to the *nai'a* bunk. Unfortunately, the cabin was not empty.

"Oh my God!" Sierra rushed to Danica as soon as she saw her hobble up the steps.

"Danica! What happened?" Sasha followed them all inside.

"Just a little ankle twist. I'm fine," Danica said as Micah eased her onto her bed.

"Are you sure? Can I get you something?" Sasha asked, concerned.

"No, that's okay."

"An extra pillow? A magazine? Anything?" she offered.

"It's fine," Danica said.

"Some snacks?" Sasha went on. "I think I have some of those yucca chips that you like."

"Don't worry. I'm *fine*," Danica repeated. She glanced at Micah and then gave Sierra a look that said, *Get her out of here!*

Sierra nodded. "Sash, I think they've got it covered," she whispered.

"Ohhhhhh," Sasha said, finally getting it. "Wait.

I just remembered. We have to go. We've got, um, *stuff*." She nudged Sierra. *"Right?"* She never was one for subtleties.

Sierra rolled her eyes. "Yeah. Let's go."

"I guess I'll head out, too," Micah said. "You sure you don't want anything?"

Danica wanted a lot of things, but she settled for ice. "Would you be a sweetie and get me some ice from the mess hall?" she asked him.

Micah nodded. "I'll be back."

I know, Danica thought. And by then she'd have an excuse for him to stay and they'd talk about old times—fun times—and he'd forget all about Cassie Hamilton.

Poor thing. She'll be so upset.

Danica knew she was probably right. But she slid her cell phone off her nightstand and began to text a message—just to make sure:

Did you hear? Cassie's leaving camp tomorrow for good to cram for the Brazil qualifiers with her coach.

Maybe it was manipulative or playing dirty or even completely wrong by average standards, especially since she was texting Emmy, the camp

78

gossip. But Danica didn't care. Hopefully Micah would not be happy about being the last to know, and then he'd pick a fight, and maybe Cassie really *would* leave.

All's fair in love and surfing, she thought, just as she clicked Send.

Four

"Lance? What do you call that thingy us surfers do when we hang our toes over the front edge of a long board?" Tori asked at the campfire later that night.

"Hang ten?"

"Oh, riiiiiight." Tori giggled. "You're so smart."

Lance wrinkled his nose. "You know how to do a cheater five but you don't know what hang ten is? How is that possible?"

"Oh, um, I was just *testing* you, silly." Tori slapped him playfully on his beefy arm. "And you totally passed. Congratulations!"

"Thanks!" Lance swung his right arm around Tori and gave her a squeeze. "Do I win a prize?"

"Okay." Tori gave him a peck on the cheek.

Cassie switched her position on the log she was sharing with Lance and Tori, marveling at her cousin's flirting skills. *Tori should definitely make her own infomercial*, she thought, staring into the fire pit a few yards away. *Girls across America could use her help—me included*.

While Lance turned away to chat with the Peewee bunk's counselor, Jack, Tori leaned in to Cassie. "Why, oh *why* does Lance have to be so *hot*?" she whispered. "It's *so* not fair."

"Let me get this straight," Cassie said. "You're *complaining* because the guy you've got wrapped around your pinky is *too* cute. Isn't that a little warped?"

"No." Tori slumped her shoulders. "Eddie is really cute, too, and, well, you saw what Sam looks like," she whispered. "They're all equally sweet and funny and they *all* like me."

"Poor baby," Cassie said sarcastically.

"I'm serious, Cass. It's a major problem. And they don't know about each other. How am I supposed to choose one if they're all awesome?"

"Why do you have to?" Cassie asked.

Tori shrugged. "A girl can juggle three boys only for so long. A decision needs to be made—soon. I can feel it."

"Hmm." Cassie tapped her fingers on her chin. Finally she said, "Pick Lance. I mean, he's right here, isn't he?" She was only kidding, but Tori seemed to seriously consider it.

"Well . . . he *is* the cutest," Tori said after a few seconds. "Okay. From this moment forward, I am a one-guy girl. And Lance is the one. Problem solved. Thanks, Cass!" She hooked arms with Lance and whispered something in his ear that Cassie couldn't hear.

Tori, a one-guy girl? Cassie guessed it was possible, but she wasn't betting money on it. She sipped from the cup of fruit punch she was holding as she took in the scene around her. To her left, some of the younger girls were singing along to an old Britney Spears song playing from the canteen. A group of boys, hovering around the grill, scarfed down hot dogs and hamburgers. Cassie eyed the snack table set up with chips and pretzels and cookies. *I need marshmallows*, she thought. *What good is a campfire without marshmallows?*

But instead of marshmallows she spotted Andi and Charlie sitting on a log on the other side of the pit, huddled deep in conversation, and wondered if they were on their first official date.

Which made Cassie think about *her* date. Where was he?

Lance leaned across Tori. "Hey, Cassie. What's Micah up to?"

"Yeah. When's he getting here?" Tori asked. "I thought we could all go for a walk by the beach later."

"I don't know." Cassie glanced at her watch. It was almost eight. Cassie thought they'd be cuddling in front of the fire by now. A dreamy walk on the beach sounded good, too. Plus she wanted to get Micah's take on training for Brazil. "Maybe I should go look for him."

Almost as soon as she said this, Charlie seemed to materialize by her side. "Hi, Cassie."

"What's up? Got any good news for me?" she asked him, hoping he'd say that he and Andi were dating now. She gazed across the pit expecting to see Andi still on the log, but two girls in blue Camp Ohana T-shirts had taken her place.

"Not really news, but I came by to tell you *something*," Charlie said. Then he leaned in and whispered. "Good luck in Brazil."

Brazil? How'd he know about that? Cassie hadn't told anyone about it yet. Not even Tori.

Charlie must have noticed her mouth stuck in the open, shocked position. "Don't worry. I'm not mad at you for not telling me. Well, I was at first, but now I guess I'm okay with it. Oh, and your secret is safe. I won't tell a soul."

"Won't tell a soul what?" Tori asked.

"That Cassie's going to a surfing competition in Brazil." Charlie slapped a hand over his mouth, then removed it and smiled sheepishly. "Um, I'm just gonna leave now—get some punch. Anybody need a refill?"

"No, but you can get us some marshmallows. Thanks," Cassie said, fuming.

"Will do," Charlie replied and then he was gone.

Tori stared at Cassie. "Since when are you going to Brazil?"

Cassie opened her mouth to answer, when Andi came striding over. "Oh, good. You're still here. I want you to have this." She shoved a pretty pink and yellow friendship bracelet into Cassie hand. "I didn't want you to sneak out of here without getting to say good-bye."

"*Good-bye?*" Cassie repeated. "Who told you I'm going anywhere?"

84

"I know." Andi touched a hand to her chest. "I'm not good at these things, either. But the bunk won't be the same without you." She bent down and gave Cassie a big hug, then pulled back, wiping away a few stray tears. "I'm so mad at you. I can't believe you're leaving tomorrow!"

"But—" Cassie said.

Andi held up a hand to stop her. "Let's talk later tonight. Okay? Or else I'm going to totally bawl in public."

"Um . . ." Cassie watched her race-walk away.

"You're quitting camp!" Tori cried when she was gone.

Lance turned to Tori. "Somebody's quitting camp?"

"No! I mean, I don't know if I am." Cassie sighed. "Kiera suggested it earlier today, but I didn't give her an answer." How could she? There was so much to consider, like Micah, for one, and Tori, and the commitment she made to Simona, and . . . Micah. "How does everybody know about my plans before I've even made them?"

"You should ask around," Tori said icily. "But don't ask me, 'cause apparently I'm the last to know *anything.* Don't worry. Lance and I will keep your seat warm. Maybe."

"Tori, don't be mad . . ." Cassie began.

Tori gazed away. Then her face blanched. "Uh . . . on second thought, maybe I *will* join you. What kind of cousin would I be if I didn't help, right? Let's go now, okay?"

Cassie was confused until she followed Tori's line of sight. Across the way she could see Eddie waving and walking toward their log from the left side of the campfire, while at the same time, Sam was smiling and heading over from the right side. Any second, all three of Tori's boyfriends would be in the same six-foot radius.

Cassie grabbed Tori's hand and pulled her to her feet. "Be right back, Lance. We've got to go do some girl stuff." And they disappeared into the crowd.

It took about twenty minutes for Tori to find out that Andi had gotten the news from Charlie, who had found out from Haydee, the girls' surfing counselor, who'd talked about it with Neil, who couldn't remember who had mentioned it to him . . . a camper maybe.

"A camper?" Tori folded her arms across her chest. "Cassie, how could some random camper know before your own flesh-and-blood camper?"

"I swear, Tori. I was going to tell you—just as soon as I figured out what I was doing," Cassie said.

Tori pouted. "Well, it doesn't matter, anyway, since most of camp probably knows by now."

"True," Cassie agreed. Then a horrible thought entered her brain. "Oh my God."

"What?" Tori asked.

Cassie started down the path toward the boys' bunks. "I'll meet you back by the fire pit, okay? I have to find Micah. Like, right now."

If Tori and Andi and Charlie had been insulted not knowing about the rumor, Cassie could only imagine how her boyfriend might feel. Cassie didn't want Micah to think that she'd leave Camp Ohana without saying good-bye. Not even for a minute.

'Cause she'd never do that.

No way.

* * *

"Shoot," Micah muttered when he realized it

was dark outside. He quickly closed the door to the *nai'a* bunk and jogged down the steps.

Micah didn't know how it had happened, but he'd ended up spending the rest of the day with Danica, reminiscing about the crazy things they'd done last summer, like the time when, on a dare, they both dived off the edge of No Man's Return into the lagoon, then got kitchen duty for a week for sneaking off the Ohana beach to do it. He'd totally lost track of time and now he was late meeting Cassie at the campfire.

He started up the path, which was edged with glowing solar lanterns.

"Hey, Sims. Wait up!" he heard Ben calling from behind him.

Micah stopped and turned. "What's up?"

Ben approached him holding a box filled with bags of marshmallows, graham crackers, chocolate, and a bunch of skewers. "Shouldn't I be asking you that question?" he said with a smirk. "You and Cassie *and* you and Danica? Hanging out with two girls from the same bunk, huh? I'm impressed."

Micah laughed. "You've got it all wrong. Danica and I are just friends."

"No man, I get it," Ben said, and nudged him. "Cassie's leaving camp tomorrow, so you're trying to talk to Danica again. No shame in that. She's hot."

"I'm not trying to get with Danica." Micah's mind spun. "Wait. Did you say Cassie's leaving camp tomorrow? She's not."

"That's not what I heard," Ben said. "I heard her bags are packed and her coach is coming to pick her up tomorrow. She's supposed to fly to some competition in Japan or Argentina or something. I don't know."

"You're wrong," Micah said, shaking his head. He was sure of it. Cassie would definitely have told him.

"Don't think so, buddy," Ben said.

Just then Charlie ran past them. He stopped when he noticed the box Ben was holding and backtracked. "Ben, my man, people are *calling* for the marshmallows. " He snatched a bag of them. "I've got to get these to the campfire before there's a riot."

Ben grabbed Charlie's arm. "Wait a sec. Have you heard that thing about Cassie leaving? She's going to Tahiti, right?"

"No way," Charlie said, and Micah exhaled. He knew she wouldn't just *leave* without telling him.

But then Charlie glanced over both of his shoulders and said, "She's not going to Tahiti . . . she's going to this big surfing competition in Brazil. But if she asks, you didn't hear it from me. See you guys later. She's already mad that I told Andi."

"Sure." Micah swallowed hard.

So it was true.

He still didn't want to believe it—that Cassie was bailing on camp . . . and on him. But she was.

How could Cassie do this? She knew how much he liked her. There were feelings involved.

But, right now, all he was feeling was played.

Micah stood by the fire pit a little while later, skewer in his hand, feeling stupid. Partly because his own girlfriend didn't tell him that she was leaving and that he might never see her again, and partly because he was the only guy among a sea of eleven-year-old girls toasting marshmallows.

He pulled his skewer out of the fire to reveal a black burnt glob on the end—just how he liked it. When he blew on the glob to cool it off, it slipped off the skewer and splattered onto the ground next to his last three attempts.

"You keep cooking it too long," the little redhead next to him explained. "Gets too mushy." She angled her skewer toward Micah. "Here."

"Thanks." Micah slipped off the marshmallow and popped it in his mouth.

That was when he saw Cassie. She was chatting with her cousin Tori and a camper named Lance who was in the advanced surfing class. Micah wanted to go over there, but he hesitated, feeling weird. What was he supposed to say? *Nice knowing you? Bon voyage? Happy trails?*

A few minutes later Micah spotted Danica quickly weaving through the crowd. Her ankle must have been feeling better because she wasn't limping anymore, which was cool. It was also kind of cool that she had said nice things about Cassie earlier—almost as if the girls had become friends.

But when Micah observed Cassie stopping Danica, mid-weave, to begin a friendly conversation, he wondered if maybe their newfound friendship *wasn't* so cool. It was a known fact that a girl's favorite pastime was talking—about people—and

Cassie and Danica seemed as if they were in a serious discussion. What were they saying? He hoped they weren't comparing notes about him. That would be bad.

Stop being paranoid, Micah told himself, and stabbed another marshmallow onto his skewer. Moments later he peeked at them again, trying not to be obvious about it. Apparently Ben had inserted himself into the exchange now, only it seemed as if Cassie had fallen out of the conversation.

Micah watched her gaze into the fire pit . . . smile at Charlie, who was now planted on a boulder, strumming on a guitar and singing off-key . . . lock eyes onto him . . .

Micah swallowed hard as she smiled and waved and headed over. *Be cool.*

"What are you doing over here?" Cassie asked.

Micah shrugged. "Toasting marshmallows." He pulled his skewer out of the fire and watched the black-and-white blob immediately plop to the floor. "Crap," he muttered.

Cassie laughed. Which made Micah laugh. Which broke the tension.

She grabbed a couple of marshmallows from a

bag and handed one to Micah. "So . . . want to go for a walk?"

"Let's go." Micah popped the raw marshmallow into his mouth.

Cassie laced her fingers into Micah's and they strolled down the beach under the light of the moon, leaving the crowd behind. Once they were well away from the party, Cassie looked up at Micah and said, "I kind of wanted to talk to you about something."

"You mean, about Brazil." Micah's body tensed. "I know."

"So you heard about that," Cassie said. She shook her head. "I am so annoyed. Somebody started the rumor about me quitting camp and it's not true." Her face was earnest.

"Really?" Micah asked. He wasn't sure if he felt relieved or a bit embarrassed that he'd assumed the worst. Maybe a little of both.

"No, it's not," Cassie told him. "I mean, there *is* a competition coming up in Brazil and Kiera wants me in Oahu for some intensive training for the qualifiers, but I never *said* that I would go. I haven't given her an answer yet." She sighed. "I have a feeling

Danica's behind this. I tried to get her to admit it, but she won't."

"Oh." If Micah wanted to, he could totally vouch for Danica, since he'd been hanging out with her alone in her bunk up until about twenty minutes ago. *Ah, maybe you should keep that info to yourself,* he decided, even though nothing shady happened—or would ever happen. It had taken a while to get there, but he and Danica were friends now. Nothing more.

Micah led Cassie to a spot near the water's edge. She sat in the sand, Indian style, and he parked himself next to her and watched the moonlight glimmer on the lapping sea. Finally he asked, "So how come you didn't give Kiera an answer?"

"Because I wanted to talk to you first. Get your take. I mean, they're this Friday. I'd have to leave right away," she said as if it was the obvious answer. "And . . ." Her voice trailed off.

"What?"

"Well, maybe I don't want to go to Brazil this year," Cassie said. "I mean, camp will be over soon and I'm not exactly ready to compete, anyway. Maybe I should just . . . take a pass on this round. I know it's a risk skipping out on Brazil but—"

"Seriously," Micah said. "I mean, I definitely don't want to see you go," he started, taking Cassie's hand. "But isn't it a huge opportunity?"

Cassie snuggled herself into the crooks of his body and exhaled. "I guess every competition is a potential opportunity. You just better make sure you're ready for it if you win."

"I don't think I'd mind winning a pro contest or two." Micah leaned back on his elbows. "For the glory of it. And . . . oh, yeah. And the endorsements."

"The glory part is awesome. I have to admit that," Cassie said. "Unfortunately, the other part? Not so glorious—depending on how you see things."

"You're getting paid to surf." Micah turned on his side toward her. "How can that possibly be bad?"

Cassie leaned back, then shifted to face Micah. "It's not, but . . . okay. It's like this. When you have a company sponsoring you, well, it's a lot of pressure," she told him. "They expect you to train hard and to win *all* the time. They say they care about you, but even if all you need is a little downtime, forget it. There are television appearances to be made and photo shoots to be done and tons of live appearances—and you'd better do it with a smile. And if you have a bad streak because, say, maybe you're tired from all the extra stuff or you came this close to the jaws of a shark, well, too bad. They can pull your funding and you can kiss surfing in the big leagues *sayonara*," she said.

"Whoa," Micah said. "Surfing shouldn't be so stressful." How could he put this delicately? "Maybe you should just . . . loosen up about it."

"Loosen up," Cassie repeated. "Am I *that* tense?"

"Kinda . . ." Micah said, gently. But who could blame her? "I have an idea . . ." He paused to gather his thoughts. "I know it sounds crazy, but you've been stressing about getting back on the board since you got here. You haven't had a chance to chill at all. What if you prepared for the qualifiers by *not* thinking about them at all? Stopped pressuring yourself?" he asked. "I bet you'd just go out there on Friday and rock those qualifiers. Like you said, sometimes all you need is a little downtime."

"It's that easy?" Cassie seemed doubtful.

"I don't know if it is," Micah admitted. He slid his hand into hers and played with her fingers.

"But, Cassie, I saw you surf last year at the Ohana expo. I know you love it. You shouldn't throw away everything you've worked for because of a setback. Anyway, it's just a suggestion."

Cassie considered it for a moment. "Well . . . I guess forcing myself back into competition mode hasn't exactly been working out for me. Maybe it's worth a try, only . . ." Cassie leaned closer, her face only inches from his. "Surfing is my life, Micah. How am I supposed to *not* think about it? Do you have any more suggestions?" Her blue eyes sparkled as she smiled.

"I can think of some," Micah replied just before they kissed.

Five

"Abby, tomorrow we're catching some bigger waves," Danica informed her eleven-year-old student at the end of the girls' beginner group lesson. "These little ones are for beginners and you, my girl, are no longer a beginner." A feeling of pride swelled inside her. To think, only a few weeks ago, this girl was afraid to stand on her board in shallow water. Danica had almost given up on her, but she was glad that she hadn't.

Sitting on the sand, Abby unleashed herself from the red Ohana surfboard. "Are you sure I'm ready?" she asked as if she were not convinced.

"Is the sky blue?" Danica asked.

"Nope. It's blue and *white*. Lots of clouds today." Abby giggled.

"Smart aleck." Danica laughed and tussled

the girl's wet hair. "Get out of here. I'll see you tomorrow."

As Danica helped Haydee, one of the surfing counselors, gather the rest of the girls out of the water, she noticed Micah and Cassie walking hand-in-hand over to the jetty. *So much for my attempt at breaking them up.*

"*There* she is!" Ben said, stepping into her path and interrupting her thoughts.

Danica stopped. "Ben, is there a *reason* you only refer to me in the third person?" she asked, annoyed.

Ben ignored her question. "So I'm ready for my first surfing lesson."

"I don't remember offering one," Danica retorted, and started up again.

"Oh, you didn't say it so much with words as with your *eyes*," Ben replied, chasing behind her.

What a jerk. "Nice talking to you, Ben," Danica said. She waved her hand back and forth. "Go away."

"Aw, come on, Danica. Let's go swimming, then," Ben said. "I'll race you."

"*Busy*. I have to go pick the lint off my bedspread," Danica added, leaving him behind.

"Guess you're afraid I'll beat you, huh?"

Danica stopped again. Beat *her*? Ben spent his days rowing a plastic tub. Danica, on the other hand, was *in* the ocean every day conquering the surf. There was no *way* that meathead could *ever* beat her in a swimming contest. She leaned her board against the wooden wall of the girls' showers and turned to face him. "Fine. If you really want to embarrass yourself, who am I not to grant your wish?"

Ben grinned. "We'll see," he said, following her to the water's edge.

Danica gestured to a red buoy bobbing in the ocean about twenty yards away. "We'll race to there."

"Too easy," Ben said. "Let's go to that one." He pointed to the one way off to the right.

Danica squinted at it in the distance. "If you're okay with it, I'm okay with it." She was strong enough to make it there. "But if you get into trouble, let me know."

"You too. Go!" He ran into the water.

"Hey!" Danica raced after him to catch up. She dove in and swam as if her life depended on it. But when she reached the buoy, Ben was already there—

granted, he was breathing much more heavily than she was. "Cheater."

"Guilty," Ben said between breaths. "Why . . . aren't . . . you tired?"

Danica surveyed Ben's face as she took hold of the buoy. He didn't look so hot. Actually, the boy looked hot, but not as hot as he usually looked. "Are you okay?" she asked.

"Just need to rest . . . a minute."

"Okay," Danica said, but she doubted if he could make it back all the way to camp. There was a parasailing dock nearby, which was a lot closer. "You want to swim to there, then walk back on the beach?" she asked Ben.

To her surprise he nodded yes. A few minutes later they were slowly making their way to the dock.

"You're a great swimmer," he told Danica.

"You're a great *cheater*," Danica replied. She splashed him with some water even though she wasn't really mad about it.

Soon they arrived at the cement dock and were climbing the metal rungs attached to it. When they emerged from the water, a guy in his twenties carrying a clipboard was there to greet them at the foot of the dock.

"We've got the tandem equipment all ready, Ben," the guy said.

"Thanks, Huey," Ben replied as if he knew him, which he obviously did since he called him by name.

Danica glanced at the idling speedboat, then at the two other guys laying out the huge yellow-and-red-and-blue parachute on the beach, then at Ben. "You tricked me," she said.

Ben shrugged and gave her a boyish smile. "You said you wanted to go parasailing."

"No, I didn't." Danica folded her arms across her chest. "I never said anything. 'Cause you never *asked* me."

"I didn't?" he said. "Oh, my bad. You want to go parasailing?" There was that boyish grin again.

Danica had never been parasailing before. She kind of wanted to do it, now that they were there, but she didn't want to make it easy for Ben. "Okay, but only if we can go separately." She looked at the guy with the clipboard. "Huey? Can you make it happen?"

"No can do," Huey said. "We only have time for a tandem."

"Come on, Danica. It'll be fun," Ben said.

"Fine. I'll do it," she said. "For the *experience*—not because I want to be harnessed to *you*."

Huey led them down the dock, and before Danica knew it she and Ben were strapped together and attached to the parachute, which was attached to the speedboat. The boat chugged away from the dock, then zoomed from shore. Danica and Ben ran down the beach toward the water until the parachute caught air. A moment later, they were flying!

"Yes! I love this!" Danica cried as her stomach dropped from the rush of the quick ascent. She turned her head slightly to see Ben, who was behind her. "This is awesome!"

"I knew you'd like it," Ben said, holding on to her waist. He kind of had to—although Danica suspected that maybe he wanted to—the way the harness was built, she was practically sitting in Ben's lap.

Danica gazed down at the crystalline green ocean, at the ribbon of white sands and volcanic rock along the Kona coastline. Never in her life had a boy put so much . . . effort into getting her to like him—not even super nice Micah.

Maybe . . . maybe I misjudged this guy, she thought.

They flew around a bend past a cluster of green palms and bright splashes of tropical wildflowers. "It's *so* beautiful," Danica breathed, leaning back into Ben, beginning to relax. "Thanks."

"You're welcome," Ben said. Then he kissed her on the cheek.

"Ben!" Danica cried, surprised, but trying to hold back her smile.

"Oh, come on. You liked it," Ben said.

"I did *not*," Danica told him.

Except . . . kinda, maybe she did.

About an hour later Danica was alone and walking back to her bunk, wondering why she never noticed the cute dimple in Ben's right cheek before.

"Ow!" a girl cried, pulling Danica's thoughts away from Ben's dimple.

"Sorry," another girl whispered. "Mosquito on your leg."

"Who's there?" Danica asked. She looked

around but didn't see anyone. Suddenly arms reached out of the huge azalea bushes behind Simona's office and pulled her in. "Whoa!"

"Shh!" Sasha put an index finger to her lips.

"They'll hear you," Sierra added.

"Who?" Danica asked. "Why are you guys hiding out in the bushes?"

"We're dying to find out if Cassie is staying or going," Sierra whispered.

"What? But I thought she was staying." Danica had assumed Cassie was the kind of girl who was too wimpy to leave her boyfriend behind.

Maybe not. She crept forward and parted the bushes. From this vantage Danica could see Simona, Cassie, and Kiera, chatting in the parking lot by Kiera's truck. Kiera was there to convince Cassie to go back to Oahu, obviously. Unfortunately Danica couldn't hear a word they were saying.

"You guys stay here," she told her friends. "I'm going in for a closer look. I'll report back with the news."

At the first chance, Danica made a break for the rear bumper of Kiera's flatbed.

"I thought if I came by in person I could change

your mind. I don't agree with your choice to train here, Cassie . . . " Kiera was saying.

I knew she wasn't going anywhere, Danica said silently.

". . . But I respect the fact that you want to fulfill your commitment to the camp," Kiera finished.

Oh. Well, that's a pretty decent reason to stay, Danica thought. *Better than a boyfriend, anyway.*

Cassie nodded. "Thanks."

"And *I* appreciate that Cassie's not leaving me shorthanded," Simona added. "Which is why I agreed to let *Surf Girl* magazine come here for the interview and photo shoot after the qualifying round."

"Coco Beach would like to ship some new gear for Cassie to wear at the shoot, if you don't mind," Kiera told Simona. "Can I give them the go-ahead?"

"That's fine," Simona said.

"So it's all set." Kiera rubbed her palms together, then clapped Cassie on the back. "You'll be ready to surf on Friday?" she asked her.

By the time Cassie promised she would be, Danica's mind was already whirring. A *Surf Girl* interview? And a photo shoot? This was a prime opportunity.

"Ommmmmmm." Eyes closed, Cassie sat cross-legged in the center of her bed with her palms resting on her knees. It was Friday morning. She had already eaten breakfast, waxed the deck of her surfboard, tried on her new Coco Beach bikini, and packed a bag containing her wet suit, sunscreen, and all the other essentials she'd need with her in Hilo later that day.

Now she was becoming one with the universe. "Ommmmmmm."

She had no idea whether or not it was working, though. At the very least she was relaxed, and wasn't that the whole point of staying at Camp Ohana instead of training with Kiera?

Cassie had taken Micah's advice and had spent the past three days *not* thinking about surfing, and Micah had been more than happy to help distract her. Every day after they finished with their C.I.T. duties, they went on a mini adventure. Tuesday it was a little hike up to the top of Lotus Point, Wednesday they went swimming in the lagoon, Thursday they climbed out onto the jetty and talked and laughed and told stupid jokes.

And of course there was tons of kissing and holding hands to keep her busy. Not once had Cassie worried about surfing or sharks or anything that wasn't warm and fuzzy. She'd even hidden her surfboard underneath her bed so she wouldn't be tempted to stress.

"Ommmmmmm."

She opened her eyes feeling rested and calm and, for the first time in a long time, ready to surf. Could it really have worked? Were a few days of relaxation all she needed to get back in the game? Cassie had to admit, she'd had her doubts in the beginning but she couldn't deny how great she felt this morning!

She scooted off of her bed, picked up the ankle bracelet that Micah had given her, and tied it around her ankle for good luck. Then she slung her duffel over her shoulder and grabbed her board. *Today I'm gonna totally bring it*, she said to herself. *I'm gonna do my coach proud. The sponsors are going to love me again. I'm going to be great!* She felt that old excitement begin to bubble as she headed out with a new sense of confidence.

Her enthusiasm doubled when she saw Micah

leaning against a palm tree outside of her bunk. "What are you doing here?"

"I wanted to wish you luck again," he said and kissed her lips. He took her board and held her hand as they walked the gravelly path. When they reached the parking lot, Kiera's truck was already there. Micah balanced the board against a wall of Simona's office and wrapped Cassie in a hug. "Good luck," he whispered. "Kick butt."

"Thanks. I will." Cassie gave him one last kiss. Then she took hold of her board and headed to the truck, stopping for a second to look back. She smiled to herself when she saw him still there. "Hi, Kiera!" she called, waving to her coach, who was sitting behind the wheel of the truck. Cassie was about to place her surfboard in the back when she spotted Danica's bright pink board already nestled comfortably in the flatbed. Her smile faded as she laid hers next to it. "How come Danica's board is in your truck?" she asked Kiera.

"Danica asked me if she could come to watch you surf . . . and maybe catch a few waves after the competition," Kiera replied. "I thought you could use the moral support."

Danica burst out of the back door to Simona's office, wearing a pink Coco Beach bikini and denim cutoffs. Her long white-blond hair was piled on top of her head. "Heyyyy!" she called to Cassie. "Are you readddddyy?"

"Yup," Cassie replied. She could think of ten other people she'd rather have come to the competition with her—like Micah, for one—but she guessed it was nice of Danica to want to encourage her.

The two-hour truck ride to Hilo was a bit cramped with Kiera driving, Danica in the middle, and Cassie in the passenger's seat, and a bit annoying with Danica yakking nonstop about surfing the big waves in Oahu—*like, who hasn't*—and how she's dying to surf-and-see another country. Danica finally stopped to take a breath when they pulled up to the Honoli'i beach.

Cassie jumped out of the truck to survey the surf. The breakers were decent but nothing near the size of the waves in Oahu. It meant that the competition would be more about technique than survival, which was fine with Cassie.

Cassie squeezed into the bottom half of her wet

suit, leaving the top part hanging open, then went to register her name and get her number. All of the usuals were there, the pros from the circuit, a couple of familiar judges, the surf enthusiasts, journalists, as well as a few faces Cassie didn't recognize. Normally, she'd be chatting casually or taking pictures with her friends before the start of the competition. Today, though, Cassie knew she needed to stay focused.

You can do this. You're a pro. You're relaxed. The surf is easy, she assured herself after she'd checked in.

She found Kiera and Danica opening up a blanket on the beach and talking with a guy in a pair of dark jeans and a polo shirt. *Jeans on the beach? Definitely not a local—or a surfer*, Cassie knew.

"Oh, Cassie. I want you to meet the new marketing executive from Coco Beach," Kiera said, waving her over. "Cassie, this is Mr. Hainsbro. Mr. Hainsbro, this is Cassie Hamilton, the face of Coco Beach."

"Nice to meet you," Cassie said.

"I'm looking forward to seeing you perform." Mr. Hainsbro shook her hand firmly. "It's hard to believe that I've been with the company for three months and I haven't seen you surf once." His lips curled into a smile, but his eyes remained stony.

Cassie felt her shoulders tense. *Is he trying to tell me something?*

"Oh, she'll be a total powerhouse out there," Kiera cut in. "She's been training super hard for her comeback."

Except that I haven't, Cassie thought. *Up until the past three days I've been too freaked about sharks to do much. And nobody said* anything *about this being my official comeback.* An invisible pin pierced the back of her neck as a tiny drip of doubt entered her mind. *Can I really do this?* she wondered, then immediately brushed away the negative thought. *Stay loose*, she reminded herself.

"Um, I should probably get ready for my run." Cassie took hold of her board, which Kiera had brought from the truck, and politely removed herself from the scene.

She waved to a few girls she had seen on the circuit, who apparently were excited about some giant jellyfish sightings seen last week, as she searched for an empty spot in the sand to chill. Cassie tried to concentrate on the waves, tried to figure out their pattern. But she couldn't stop thinking.

What if I'm not *a powerhouse? What if I totally suck? Or worse, what if I panic out there?* Cassie could already see the headlines on the surf blogs: *Once Bitten Bites it in Hilo, Hamilton's Hilo Gutted by Recent Shark Attack, Hamilton Says Buh-Bye to Brazil!*

Cut it out, Cass, she scolded herself. *Stay positive. You've done this a million times before. Remember how awesome you felt this morning?* She took a deep breath, shook out her arms, and stretched her neck from side to side trying to relax. But it wasn't coming so easily. *I wonder if there's time to call Micah for a quick pep talk.*

A whistle sounded and Cassie noticed the contestants in her heat rounding up by the edge of the water. *Guess not.* She pulled into the rest of her wet suit, zipped it up, and joined them with her board.

"Would you stop talking about those stupid man-o-war jellyfish already?" a girl named Aisha was saying. "I mean the stings kill, but there are worse things out there. Tell her, Cassie."

"Aisha! Shut up!" Julie, another surfer, said. "God, you are so dense sometimes."

By then Cassie's stomach had gone cold. The other surfers were entering the Pacific and Cassie knew she had to follow them. The moment the icy ocean swirled across her feet, Cassie felt as if her heart was seizing.

Come on. Stop this. You said you were ready. You wanted to surf. You have to. You . . . HAVE . . . to . . .

Cassie waded only a few more steps before the millions of white dots appeared before her eyes, and she knew she had reached the wall. "No. Not now. I'm barely in the water!" She tried to forge on but her head was spinning too fast!

I can't, Cassie realized. *I can't do this!* She fell to her knees, splashing the salty shallows, completely oblivious to the clicking shutters of the cameras.

And then there was the nausea, the lurch . . .

A moment later Kiera and Danica were helping her up, carrying Cassie to the sand, brushing the wet hair from her face.

"I tried," Cassie kept saying over and over. "I'm sorry. I tried . . ."

It just wasn't good enough.

Six

Danica stared in horror at a pale Cassie, who was now sitting on their blanket with her face in her hands. She kneeled next to her. "Are you . . . okay, now?"

"Just humiliated." Cassie hugged her legs toward her chest and rested her forehead on her knees, hiding her face.

And for good reason.

Cassie had caused a major scene, the contest had been paused, and now a crowd was gathering. Among the onlookers were contest officials, journalists and photographers covering the qualifiers, and Cassie's competitors. They all wanted to know the same thing Danica did.

"What happened to you?" Danica whispered.

"I . . . I don't know," Cassie said, not raising her

head. "I guess I freaked. God, I can't believe I puked in public."

"Hey, you're not the first. I'm sure you won't be the last," Danica joked. As hard as it was to believe, she actually wanted to make the girl feel better. At the moment, Cassie seemed so pathetic and alone on that blanket that Danica kind of felt a little sorry for her.

An EMT hurried over to check Cassie out. Danica didn't know what to do. She looked for Kiera and found her off to the side in what seemed to be a serious conversation with the Coco Beach man. *Uh-oh. That doesn't look good.* Moments later, the two of them were headed back to the blanket.

"How's she doing?" Kiera asked.

"Blood pressure's fine. Temperature's normal. Heart sounds good," the EMT reported. "What have you eaten recently?" he asked Cassie.

"Well, there *was* that sushi we stopped for on the way here," Kiera mentioned for her.

Only, there was no sushi. They hadn't stopped for as much as a Twinkie, let alone any real food. Danica gave Kiera a questioning look but Kiera turned to Mr. Hainsbro.

"That must be it," she told him. "Cassie's probably got a little case of food poisoning."

Kiera is covering for her, Danica realized. She had a feeling that it wasn't the first time.

"That's a good bet," the EMT said, shutting his medical box. "See how she's feeling in a few hours. If she's okay then we'll just blame it on some bad tuna roll and call it a day. I'd still like Cassie to see a doctor tomorrow, though."

"I'm *fine*," Cassie assured the EMT.

The crowd began to break. A man who looked to be a judge stepped forward and mentioned that if all was well he was going to resume the competition in a few minutes, and Kiera nodded.

"I'll speak with the head official," Kiera told Mr. Hainsbro after the judge had gone. "I'll bet I can convince him to let Cassie compete in Brazil based on past performance. They have to let her in. She's a champion, for goodness' sake!"

Cassie looked up at Kiera for a second, then buried her face in her arms again.

A champion? What kind of champion lets a coach weasel her into an international competition? Danica wondered.

The thought of it left a bad taste in her mouth. She was all about doing whatever it took to win. In surfing that meant training hard physically and mentally, playing on your opponent's weakness, psyching them out if you could. Survival of the fittest and all that.

But you have to surf! You have to get in the water, give your competition a chance to beat you. If they can't, then you're a champion. Otherwise, you're nothing but a fraud.

As far as Danica was concerned, Cassie Hamilton was a *complete* fraud! And to think, at the start of camp, Danica had felt threatened by her. *Stupid.*

"That doesn't solve the here and now, Kiera," Mr. Hainsbro was saying. "I wanted to see some Coco Beachwear in the water today. Clearly Cassie's in no condition to surf." A whistle blew and an announcement sounded for the competitors in the first heat to enter the water.

"*I'm* wearing Coco Beach," Danica spoke up suddenly. "I'll surf."

The fraud lifted her head. "Are you *kidding* me, Danica?"

Danica ignored her. She hadn't planned for this, but if Cassie wanted to waste a perfectly awesome opportunity to shine, well, fine. That didn't mean Danica had to do the same, did it? She slipped off her shorts and stood, revealing the adorable pink Coco Beach bikini that just so happened to match the color of her surfboard. She didn't even know if it was allowed, but she grabbed her board and ran to meet the others by the water before anyone could tell her not to.

Danica felt a tiny flip in her stomach as she splashed her surfboard into the sea and hopped on. She began to paddle out with the other surfers. *This is it*, she thought. *My very first pro competition!* Okay, so maybe *she* wasn't officially a pro, but she *was* surfing against professional surfers. Danica's heart almost bounced out of her chest from excitement!

"Who *are* you?" a brunette girl asked with a dumbfounded look on her face as Danica took her place at the end of the line of competitors. "You can't just squeeze into a pro competition because you feel like it."

"Don't worry about me," Danica responded. "You just worry about yourself."

"Oh, I'm not worried about anything," the girl said, "but you better not get in my way."

The comment unnerved Danica. But what did she expect—a tea party welcoming her to the club?

Calm down, she told herself. *You belong here. All you have to do is show them.* There was no time to think about the other surfers, or Cassie, or even what Kiera would say after her run.

One by one the other surfers took their turns. Danica eyed them critically, absorbing what they did well, learning from their mistakes. Before long she spotted her wave, a rising fat swell that was peaking so close she could taste it.

This was it—Danica's chance. And she was ready to take it.

Danica exhaled and cleared her mind as she felt the wave lift her board. A moment later she was dropping into the curl and Danica began to shred. Right and left, she pumped her legs so that she'd fly faster over the water.

She felt invincible, cutting back over and over until she caught some unexpected air over the lip of the wave. "Whoa!"

Danica quickly swiveled her hips, saving herself

from a wipeout by snapping her board back toward the shore, and performing a one-eighty over the crest in the process! Then she shredded through the white water until, finally, there was nothing left to surf.

It was the best ride of her life!

Danica's chest swelled as she heard the hoots and cheers from the beach. All those hours in the water, all that hard work . . . finally it was all coming together!

Kiera greeted her at the shoreline. "That was brilliant!" she cried. "You were on fire!"

Even Cassie acknowledged her with a respectful nod.

Then, over the loudspeakers, Danica heard the announcer say, "Folks, that was Danica DeLaura. She's not an official entry in the competition. But wow! She is *definitely* one to watch!"

Yes! Danica thought. Her entire body beamed with pride. *Watch me!*

If the ride to Hilo was annoying for Cassie, the journey back to Camp Ohana was torturous. It was bad enough that she'd freaked out at the beach, even worse that her bunkmate had stabbed her in the back.

But why? *Why* did Danica have to perform so flawlessly? Cassie wondered. Because the girl had been bragging about the same little aerial for *hours*—first during the rest of the competition, then during the ride to the diner, then all through lunch, then all the way back to Camp Ohana! Cassie checked her watch. A total of six hours and forty-seven minutes, to be exact.

Do the surfing gods despise me that *much?*

Finally, they were crossing underneath the familiar Camp Ohana bamboo archway, which was glowing in the evening sun. Moments later they were driving down the winding road and parking in the lot outside of the administrative hut.

The morning had begun with such promise. Cassie had been so confident she'd really surf this time. And now that Kiera was putting the truck in park, all Cassie wanted to do was go back to her bunk, crawl into her cot, and slip underneath her scratchy wool blanket.

"Well, Kiera, thanks for everything," Danica said. "This was the most amazing day of my life!"

"You did great today," Kiera responded. "You definitely have the skills and the attitude it takes to go pro."

"Oh my God. Thank you!" Danica leaned over to give Kiera a hug. "That means so much coming from you!"

Cassie felt the acid rising again in her stomach. She found the car's door handle and opened it.

"Don't go yet, Cassie," Kiera said. "We need to talk."

Uh-oh. Here it comes. The I'm-dropping-you-because-you-suck-and-I-want-to-train-your-backstabbing-friend lecture.

"Sure." Cassie slipped out of her seat, letting Danica out. Then she climbed back into the truck and pulled the door closed.

"Um, I can take your stuff in, if you want," Danica offered through the window.

Oh? The backstabber feels guilty? Cassie thought. "Whatever."

Danica gathered their things from the flatbed and disappeared down the path to the girls' bunks. All the while, Cassie felt Kiera's eyes on her but instead of meeting them with her own, she picked at an imaginary hangnail on her right index finger. Cassie wanted her coach to say something—to get it over with—but Kiera remained silent.

"I'm sorry I let you down," Cassie finally mumbled. "I don't blame you for not wanting to coach me anymore."

"Who said anything about *that*?" Kiera seemed genuinely surprised. "Yes, today was a letdown, I won't deny it, but this is about *you*, Cassie. You have to talk to me. Are you calling it quits?"

A life without surfing? The thought of it turned Cassie hollow inside. No, it wasn't what she wanted. She was sure of that much. "I don't want to quit," she said.

"Then what are we doing here?" Kiera demanded. "I can't keep making up bad sushi stories. People are going to catch on."

"Maybe not. Maybe they'll just stop eating raw fish," Cassie joked. Kiera did *not* find it funny.

"Do you think Coco Beach is going to hang around forever?" Kiera asked. "Cassie, they're talking about terminating your contract early."

At first Cassie was shocked. Then she was indignant. "Fine. Let them. If they can't understand why I'm having issues after being attacked by *a shark* . . . I mean, come on. All I need is a little time . . ."

"Let's not fool ourselves. Okay, Cassie? You've had four months. You've completely lost your confidence. I realized that today. It's time to get serious about surfing again."

Cassie knew that Kiera didn't get it. If she did, then she'd know that it was about more than a simple lack of confidence. It was about terror. Heart-pounding, knee-jittering, total-body-paralyzing *terror*. "I know, but—"

"Can I ask you a question?" Kiera interrupted her. "Did you keep up with the summer workout regimen I gave you? And the past few days, the intense workouts?"

Cassie couldn't bring herself to admit that she hadn't been surfing at all. "Um, not exactly."

"Cassie, *why*?" Kiera asked. "You know that the only way to conquer fear and doubt is through training. Seventy-five percent of surfing is mental. You *know* that. So how come you let yourself slack off?"

Maybe it was Cassie who wasn't getting it. Was she really slacking off? Was all the fear stuff an . . . excuse to slack? It couldn't be, right?

Kiera leaned back in her seat and gazed out the window. Seconds later she was smiling to herself. "Ohhhh, *I* get it. I should have expected this."

"What?" Cassie wanted to know.

"Not what. *Who*," Kiera said. "Your little boy who's a *friend*? What's his name?" She motioned out the window to Cassie's boyfriend, who had just entered the parking lot with a backpack and a blanket slung over a shoulder. He spotted Cassie and Kiera in the truck and waved.

"Micah?" Cassie replied. "He's not the problem. He's been trying to help with my surfing all summer."

"I'll bet," Kiera said with a smirk. "I should have never agreed for you come here. I should have *insisted* you train with me in Oahu this summer. You would have been over your fear by now and you'd be in top shape to compete in Brazil."

"You don't know that for sure," Cassie countered. "Maybe I needed to relax—to *not* think about surfing for a minute! Did you ever consider *that*?"

"Did your *friend* tell you that?" Kiera asked, which really irritated Cassie because, well, Kiera was right. Forgetting about surfing for a while had been Micah's idea.

"Look," Kiera went on. "A surfer's career is pretty short. You'll have plenty of time for distractions *after* you move on. Right now, you need to focus."

Micah was not a distraction. He was Cassie's boyfriend! "Like you did?" she shot back. "Weren't you dating your husband, Jon, when you won the Triple Crown?"

Kiera narrowed her eyes. "That's *different*," she said. "Jon was a serious surfer. We trained together. We were on the same circuit. He pushed me to be a better athlete and I did the same for him."

"Well, Micah is a serious surfer, too. He wants to go pro," Cassie said, defending him. Although she had to admit that neither of them had done much surfing lately. But that was all her fault. Wasn't it?

"If he was so serious about going pro," Kiera said, "he'd be practicing right now. The waves are prime."

Instead he was headed over to the truck, looking really cute with that megawatt smile on his face. "Hey, Cassie." He leaned in through the window and gave her a quick peck on the cheek. "Hi, Kiera. Mind if I steal her away? We've got some important business to take care of."

Cassie wrinkled her nose. "We do?"

"Trust me," Micah said.

"Oh, believe me. She does," Kiera murmured, then shooed Cassie out of the car.

Micah opened the door for her and she hopped out. Cassie wasn't sure if he was ignoring Kiera's comment or if he hadn't heard it.

"Do you need me at the photo shoot tomorrow?" Kiera asked. "It's no problem. I'll be here on Big Island for a while visiting family."

"Nope. I've done it before. I'll be fine," Cassie said. Actually, she didn't feel like getting into it with her coach again tomorrow. Suddenly exhausted, she slammed the car door shut. It had been a long day. "Bye, Kiera."

Kiera turned over the ignition. "Think about what I said, Cassie. You don't want to lose everything over nothing." Then she pulled away.

"What was that all about?" Micah slipped his arm around Cassie's waist.

Cassie did the same to him and rested her head on his shoulder. "Long story," she said. "Anyway, I'm too tired to think."

"Are you too tired for a picnic?" Micah gestured to the backpack. "We're all set to celebrate."

"A picnic? That's so sweet!" Cassie said. "But, um, there isn't much to celebrate. I kind of didn't surf."

Micah's jaw dropped. "But you said you were ready."

"Guess I was wrong." Cassie tried to shrug it off, but her lower lip began to quiver. She'd been holding it back all day. She didn't want to lose it now.

"Oh, man." Micah wrapped her into a hug so tight and warm that Cassie felt as if she were in a cocoon. It felt so nice in there. She wouldn't have minded staying a while. "Come on," he said a few minutes later. "Let's eat. And then you can tell me what happened."

Cassie wasn't in the mood to talk. She was beat. Plus she had a lot to process after her chat with Kiera. But Micah was being so caring and boyfriendy and had gone through all the trouble to plan the picnic.

Reluctantly, Cassie followed Micah to a private spot way down the beach, where he laid down the blanket and proceeded to pull out a couple of sandwiches, napkins, some grapes, cheese and crackers, and a thermos filled with lemonade.

Before long, the food was half eaten and Cassie had told Micah the whole horrible story—about how she'd freaked out the moment her foot had touched the water, about throwing up in front of everyone and Kiera lying about Cassie having food poisoning. She told him about Danica jumping in and surfing even though she hadn't been entered in the race, and finally, that Coco Beach was now rethinking Cassie's sponsorship.

"Whoa. Rough day." Micah scooted behind Cassie and rubbed her shoulders.

Cassie exhaled, enjoying the massage underneath the orangey sunset. The stress of the day began to melt into the sand. "It was," she said. "Awful."

After a few minutes, though, Micah began to chuckle.

"What?" Cassie asked. She could use a good laugh.

"It's *so* like Danica to push her way into a surfing competition," Micah said, shaking his head. "I mean, if anybody can do it, she can." He laughed harder.

Cassie sat up. "And you think that's a *good* thing?" she asked, kind of irritated. Shouldn't he be angry with Danica like she was? "I think it's kind of shady."

"Oh, Danica is harmless," Micah said. "She's just trying to claw her way to the top like she always does. Come on. Lean back, relax."

"Isn't that how I got into this mess in the first place?" Cassie muttered under her breath, but immediately wished she hadn't.

"Huh? What'd you say?"

"Nothing."

"You said something," Micah insisted. "You think you're in this mess because I said you should *relax*?"

"Well, if you *knew* what I said, then why did you even ask me?" *And why did I just say that?* "I'm sorry, Micah. I didn't mean to snap at you. I'm just tired and cranky."

"Okay," Micah said, though Cassie could tell that he was still upset. "But there's got to be a little bit of truth in what you said, or else you never would have said it."

Cassie didn't like where this conversation was

headed, but she could tell that Micah wasn't about to back down. "It's just . . . that I've been doing all this relaxing when I should have probably been surfing," she said gently.

"Did you blame *me* for what happened to you today?" Micah asked. "Is that why Kiera was giving me the stink eye earlier?"

"Was she?" Cassie said, although she'd noticed it, too. "Besides, how could I blame you? You've done nothing but help me, Micah."

That *was* what she'd told Kiera, and it seemed to put him as ease. At least she thought it had until Micah said, "So . . . what does your coach have against me, anyway?"

"Nothing. Really," Cassie said. *Except that she thinks you're a distraction and ruining my career.*

"Come on, Cass. I know she doesn't like me. She pretty much said so in the truck today. What's the problem?"

Cassie hesitated. She knew she'd be opening up a can of worms if she told him. But she had no choice. "Well, it's no biggie. I mean, Kiera just thinks a boyfriend is . . . a little bit of a distraction for me, that's all."

"And what do you think?" he asked.

"I think you're a very *cute* distraction." Cassie leaned in for a kiss, hoping it would distract *Micah* from the current subject. And it did for a few moments, but then he got distracted from the kissing.

Micah gave her a final kiss on the lips before turning to look at the sea. "Your coach is a real piece of work. So, Kiera doesn't want you to have a boyfriend. Like, *ever*? That's kind of dumb." He scoffed and shook his head.

"Kiera's *not* dumb," Cassie said. *Unreasonable, yes. Dumb, no.* "She just wants me to consider my career first before guys. Or at least date a surfer."

Micah raised his hand and waved it. "Hello? Surfer?"

"Yeah, but not a *real* surfer," Cassie replied. *Oops.*

"What?"

"I mean you're not a *professional* surfer. I didn't mean you're not real. You're *very* real. I used the wrong word."

Micah folded his arms across his chest. "Or maybe you didn't."

"No. I totally did. Besides, Kiera only said that because she thinks a pro would push a pro to do better. She's got nothing against you personally," Cassie said, trying to explain. "She's got a lot of time invested in me so maybe she's a little overprotective. She doesn't want anything to hold me back."

"Hold you back," Micah repeated. "You think I hold you *back*?"

"I didn't mean that," Cassie began. She didn't, did she?

But Micah wasn't listening. "Aren't you the one who hasn't been able to get on her board all summer? Me? I've been doing great. I came in third at the intercamp competition. You remember that, don't you?"

"Of course I do, Micah," Cassie said, trying to take his hand, but he pulled it away.

"You know what I just realized?" Micah said. "I've barely surfed at all since I started seeing *you*." He stood, brushed the sand off his shorts. "I've been too busy holding your hand every time you get into the water. If anyone's been held back this summer, it's me!"

Cassie felt as if Micah had plunged a knife into her heart. She gazed away from him, at the crashing sea as her eyes blurred with tears.

I didn't mean what I said, but he's so hurt. And now he wants to hurt me!

When she found to courage to look back she realized he was walking away.

"Micah! Wait!" Cassie shouted after him. "Please! Where are you going?"

"Away from *you*." Micah turned but continued walking. "Maybe you should date a *real* surfer. I wouldn't want you to lose everything over nothing!"

Tears burning her cheeks, Cassie watched as he disappeared around the dunes. She didn't want to lose everything over nothing, either, but somehow . . .

I think I just did.

Seven

"Hey, Micah! I have to ask you something!" Ben called out from the lanai of the mess hall. "Where're you going?"

Micah blew past the building without a word, too upset to talk to anybody. What was he feeling? Embarrassed, hurt, angry? Like his heart was being ripped from his chest? Like he'd wasted his entire summer?

All of the above?

I can't believe *she thinks I'm not a real surfer!* Micah bounded the stairs to his bunk. He wasn't buying the whole wrong-word excuse. Cassie had been off guard when she'd said it, and if Micah knew one thing, it was that the truth almost *always* came out when a person was off guard.

Micah sat on his bed and raked a hand through

his hair. The thing was, he'd always felt weird because Cassie was a pro surfer and he wasn't. Part of him thought that maybe she'd look down on him a little because he wasn't at the top of his game yet. Another part thought it was just his own little insecurity and that he should get over it. Then when Cassie had asked him to help her, he was like, *Wow. She respects my surfing that much? Cool!*

But Cassie didn't value him much at all, did she?

Not a real surfer . . . The words kept stinging his ears. He could understand them coming from Kiera—she didn't know him—but Cassie? After everything Micah did for her?

He almost wished that he'd never heard her say those words, that he didn't know the truth. But he did. How could he look her in the face, how could he hold her in his arms when he knew how she really felt about him?

Micah stood and began pacing the room. Maybe if he'd helped Cassie—really helped her get back on her board—it would have never come to this. *Why did I tell her to stop thinking about surfing? I should have pushed her. I should have told her to go train with her coach* . . . He stomped across the room, and leaned his head on a top bunk.

I should stop caring, he told himself. *But I can't.*

Micah needed to do something. He needed to clear his head of all this drama, to forget about Cassie or risk going nuts. He slid his short board out from underneath his bed, grabbed a wet suit, and headed out.

He was going to surf. He was going to do what he'd planned on doing every day this summer—before he'd met Cassie.

When he reached the beach, his heart sunk to an even lower rung. Someone had posted red flags in the sand, which meant that the water wasn't safe to enter right now.

"Figures." He briefly considered going in, anyway, but decided it wasn't worth the risk.

He wandered down the beach but then stopped in his tracks when he saw Cassie and her cousin Tori in the distance. Cassie was hunched and covering her face. Tori had a hand on Cassie's arm and, from what Micah could tell, a concerned expression on her face.

Is Cassie crying? Did I make her cry? Micah felt awful. His stomach twisted into a knot. His heart told him to run down the beach, to take her in his arms and apologize so that she wouldn't cry anymore, but his head said, *Stop caring.*

Seeing her, his mixed-up feelings . . . it was all so confusing.

Micah turned away and walked in the opposite direction. He walked and walked. He walked down the length of the beach until he could walk no farther. Then he turned back and walked home, barely registering that the stars had replaced the sun.

The darkness seemed to calm him. The sound of the surf untied the jumble in his mind. By the time Micah returned back to Camp Ohana he felt peaceful and centered.

He knew exactly what he wanted to do.

He hiked up the beach, then toward the path for the girls' bunks. Moments later he was standing in front of the *nai'a* bunk—Cassie's bunk. He ascended the stairs, rested his surfboard on the banister of the lanai. A few steps later he was standing in front of the door.

Micah hesitated, his hand poised to knock. Was

he sure he wanted to do this? Did he really want to put himself out there again—after everything that had happened?

Yes, he did.

Who knew whether or not it would make him feel better, but at least it was worth a shot. He cleared his throat and rapped on the door. He heard a fumble with the knob and then the door cracked open, revealing Danica wearing a pair of shorts and a tank.

"Micah?" she whispered, stepping outside in her bare feet, closing the door behind her. She seemed surprised to see him there.

But for Micah it was an obvious choice. "Hey, Danica," he said. "You're just the person I wanted to see."

Danica yawned as she carried her board to the beach early the next morning. She snagged her favorite spot in the sand, stretched her arms over her head, and yawned again. Exhausted, she fixed her gaze out onto the ocean.

Last night was so weird. Danica had been stunned to find Micah at her doorstep, to put it mildly, and slightly amused to find he had come to see her. But then she'd thought, *Of course he came to see me.*

Unfortunately, he'd also come to whine about Cassie—practically *all night*—even though they were sitting under a full moon and brilliant stars, listening to the romantic lull of the ocean.

Sure, it was nice that Micah felt comfortable enough to go to Danica for advice, but come on, did he seriously think she wanted to hear four whole hours of *waa, waa, waaaaaa*? Seriously?

In the end Danica told him to talk to his girlfriend already—not because she suddenly liked Cassie or wanted Micah's relationship with the girl to work out—she just wanted him to shut up.

Actually, what she probably should have told him to do was to get a life. Why was he so worried about what Cassie thought of him? He should have been surfing, flirting, hanging out with friends. You know . . . having *fun*? Wasn't that what summer was all about?

By now, Danica was beyond bored with Micah.

She used to think he was like an old comfy sweater, but now she realized he was more like a wet rag—despite his totally *sick* abs.

Danica would certainly have been more motivated to steal Micah and complete Operation: Destroy Cassie if there had been a better reward at the end. Say, scoring a guy like . . . Ben, for instance. Her mind drifted back to parasailing—to how exciting it was flying through the air in his arms. Funny how things change.

When Danica had first met Ben she'd thought he was totally arrogant, but now, after spending some time with him, she realized that he wasn't arrogant. He was just extremely confident. And Danica thought confidence was very sexy. Ben's cute dimple and full lips were an added bonus.

"I *knew* I'd find her out here," a familiar voice called to Danica as he strode down the beach.

Danica smiled, recognizing it. "Ben, *who* are you talking to?" she asked, giving him a hard time about the third-person thing, but secretly she was starting to like it.

Ben sat so close to Danica that their arms and legs touched.

Tingles zipped up and down the right side of her body, where their skin met. Danica didn't mind having him so near, but she knew Ben expected her to tease him about it. "Um, personal space, much?"

Ben's lips curled into a smile. "Oh, sorry. The beach is so crowded."

"It's empty," Danica said, holding back her grin and playing along.

"It is?" Ben pretended to look around. "Oh, wow. You're right!" He scooted over a bit. The electric bolts seemed to leap past the space between them and continued to gently prick her skin.

"So, it's a little early for you, isn't it?" Danica asked him. "What are you doing out here?"

Ben shrugged. "You told me this is your favorite time of day," he said. "How come you're not in the water yet?"

"I like to think a little first," Danica admitted.

"Cool," Ben said. "So are you thinking about something right now?"

Danica nodded. "Mmm-hmm."

"Me?" he asked.

Yes, Danica answered silently, but she wasn't

about to give herself away just yet. "I'm thinking about promises," she said instead.

"You mean like how you promised to teach me how to surf," Ben said, giving her a gentle nudge.

"Ben, I did *not* promise you that!" Danica laughed.

"You didn't?" Ben asked. "Oh. Well, now that there's no one around, I wouldn't mind learning. Come on. What do you say?" He grinned, making his dimple pop into his right cheek.

Danica smiled back at him. *He's so cute.* "All right," she agreed. "But my time is super valuable. I can't just *give* you a surfing lesson."

"So what's it worth?" Ben asked.

Danica paused. *Should I go for it? Should I put myself out there?* "A date," she said, deciding to dive right in.

Ben leaned closer. "What do you call this?" he asked.

"A surfing lesson," Danica replied plainly, which made Ben smile again.

"It's a deal," he said. "I think a date with you would be awesome."

"Good," Danica said.

"Good," Ben repeated.

And then Danica realized something crazy and strange and wonderful. Ben was about to kiss her! She felt her body leaning in to meet his, her head tilting to the right. As soon as their lips touched she forgot all about Micah and stealing him away from Cassie. Because what she was feeling right now was way better than any promise for revenge.

And besides, some promises were meant to be broken.

"Is she ready?" Cassie heard Tori ask later that morning.

"I got her to shower, but she went right back to bed. I'm kind of worried," she heard Andi reply.

Then Cassie heard the screen door to her bunk squeak open and slam shut. She heard two pairs of feet—one in overpriced wooden slides, the other in basic flip-flops—clunking and slapping over to her bed.

A moment later, the blanket was pulled off of her head.

Cassie squinted from the sudden brightness as Tori and Andi stood over her. She found the edge of her blanket, pulled it back over her head, and rolled over. "Go away."

"Cassie? Sweetie? You have to get out of bed now." Tori sat on the edge of the mattress. "The *Surf Girl* crew is here. They're setting up for your interview in the canteen and for the photo shoot on the beach. I know it's not on your list of favorite things to do after a fight with your boyfriend—"

"Fight?" Cassie asked. "How about breakup?" She felt her eyes sting, but the tears didn't come. She'd cried them all out last night.

"Think of it this way," Tori said gently, "the sooner you start the sooner it'll be over. Right?" She slowly peeled down the blanket again. "Then we can come back here and we'll pig out and talk about how stupid he's gonna look when he's bald."

"Yeah. We'll sneak into his bunk and shave his head tonight if you want," Andi said. "I've got my Lady Remington."

"Um, Andi? I meant when he's bald *some*day, like, at forty?"

"So?"

Cassie actually found herself smiling. She rolled over to face her friends. "I love you guys, you know that?"

Tori gasped when she saw her.

"What?" Cassie asked.

"Ummm." Andi went to her nightstand, grabbed a mirror, and handed it to Cassie.

"Oh." Cassie saw that her eyes were bloodshot and puffy from last night's crying, with dark circles cupping each of her lower lids. Her nose was so red, it looked like she'd bought it in a practical joke store, and her hair resembled half-wet, half-dry straw. In short, she looked about as good as she felt. "Well, they're going to fix me up for the photo shoot, anyway."

"No," Tori said, rooting through the enormous designer bag she carried on her shoulder. "You can't go to the interview like that. Andi, go get me a chair."

Andi flew out of the bunk. Seconds later she returned with a white plastic seat from the porch.

"Put it over here." Tori pointed to the area in front of Andi's nightstand. "Cassie, go sit in the chair."

By the serious expression on her cousin's face, Cassie thought it best to do as she was told.

Tori dumped the entire contents of her bag onto Andi's bed. She rooted through the stuff, then picked out a large round brush. "We're going natural chic today," Tori announced, brushing Cassie's hair until it was pin-straight and silky, then pulling it all into a high ponytail. Then Tori applied some tinted moisturizer, patted a bit of concealer onto Cassie's face, and swiped some mascara on the lashes. She completed the look with her favorite cherry lip gloss. "Voilà!"

Andi handed Cassie the mirror again and Cassie gazed at her reflection. Her eyes were still red, but her complexion was flawless. "Wow. You're good. Thanks, Tori."

"Oh, don't thank me." Tori held up the tube of concealer. "Thank Mr. Dior."

"Here's your bathing suit, Cassie." Andi handed her a sporty blue one-piece with white trim, which had come with the shipment of Coco Beach stuff days earlier.

Cassie quickly changed into it. She pulled on a pair of white shorts and slipped into her flip-flops.

"Ready?" Tori said

"Does it matter?" Cassie asked.

"Nope. Guess not," her cousin answered, and they were out the door.

When they arrived at the mess hall, lunch was in full swing. Cassie gazed around, hoping to get a glimpse of Micah—clearly to torture herself—but then she realized that he was probably still teaching the beginner surfing class.

She noticed a small section in the back of the canteen was cordoned off for the interview. Zuzu Clarkson, the *Surf Girl* features editor, was waiting for Cassie at a table overlooking the ocean along with a photographer and a cameraman who'd be videotaping them for the magazine's website.

"Good luck," Andi said.

"You're leaving?" Cassie asked, even though she knew Andi wouldn't be able to get close enough to see or hear anything.

Andi suddenly seemed nervous. "I have to, um, meet somebody. But I'll be back for the photo shoot. Okay?"

Cassie watched her friend weave through the crowd and exit the canteen. "I'll bet she's meeting

Charlie. I wonder why she didn't want to tell me. I think it's really cool that they're together now."

"Probably she doesn't want to rub it in, you know? After last night?" Tori suggested. "Anyway, I've got to go, too. I'm surfing today. Want to whip my kickbacks into shape, you know?"

"You mean cutbacks, right? And you're surfing without having your arm twisted?" Cassie asked. "Something tells me you'll be with a cute surfer."

"Shut up!" Tori slapped her arm playfully. "Actually, I want to practice my moves for Lance."

"Uh-huh." Cassie blinked. "So what does that have to do with surfing?" she asked, teasing her cousin.

"Quit it!" Tori slapped her again. "I totally like surfing now. Really!"

Cassie held up both hands. "Okay, okay!"

"You don't mind, do you, Cassie?" Tori asked. "'Cause if you need me for moral support, I'll totally skip it."

"Nah. It's okay. These things are always all the same. You know, questions about surfing technique, what I eat for breakfast, where the best surf is . . . no biggie. Take my board, if you want."

"Really? Wow. Thanks!" Tori said. "Okay, well, knock 'em dead. You'll be great, I know it! See you at the shoot later, Cass!"

Cassie waved good-bye to her cousin, then took a deep breath. What had Tori said? *The sooner I start, the sooner it's over.* She crossed over to Zuzu and the *Surf Girl* crew. "Hey!" she said, tapping Zuzu on the shoulder and trying to be as upbeat as possible.

Zuzu turned around, her wild, curly brown hair bouncing at her shoulders. "Great to see you again, Cassie!" she said, hugging her and air-kissing both cheeks. She fixed her plastic-rimmed glasses. "Ready to be grilled?"

What a joker. "Ha-ha. Go easy on me, okay?" Just as Cassie said this, she caught sight of the beach outside—of Haydee and Zeke teaching the kids how to surf.

Then she saw *him*.

Cassie gasped and quickly gazed away from the window, her heart aching. *How am I supposed to concentrate on this interview with Micah only fifty feet away? I can practically touch him!*

Cassie was dying to peek outside again, but

she willed herself not to. If she saw him again she'd probably burst into tears right in front of the crew.

"Hey. You all right?" Zuzu asked.

"Mm-hmm." Cassie nodded stiffly and took the seat opposite the editor. She smiled politely for the photographer.

"Maybe she's still recovering from *food poisoning*." The photographer smirked as an assistant clipped a tiny microphone to Cassie's bathing suit strap.

What was that supposed to mean? The guy clicked the shot just as Cassie's smile faded.

Zuzu fluffed her hair as the cameraman said, "And we're rolling! In three . . . two . . . one . . ."

"Hi, guys! I'm Zuzu Clarkson. Welcome to another edition of *Surf Girl*'s exclusive webcast. Today we're on the Big Island of Hawaii, *live*, with professional surfer and notorious shark wrestler, Cassie Hamilton!"

Live? Cassie swallowed hard. *Nobody said anything about being live.* She focused on the camera. "Oh, I wouldn't call myself *that*, Zuzu."

"Really?" Zuzu replied. "So it's true that you're quitting professional surfing?"

"No! I meant about the shark. Who told you I'm quitting?" Cassie asked. And where were the usual questions? "I'm taking the summer off from competing. But I'll be back on the surfing circuit full-time in a couple weeks." *I hope.*

Outside Cassie could hear the waves crashing. The surf must have been good. She wondered how Micah's students were doing today. But she wasn't going to look. No way.

"Oh, that's a relief." Zuzu pretended to wipe her brow. "So what happened to you yesterday at the Brazil qualifiers, Cassie? Word is you ate some bad sushi. Is it true?"

Cassie discretely crossed her fingers before she lied. "That rumor *is* true, Zuzu. Um, I think it was the tuna roll."

Not looking . . . wanna look but NOT looking outside . . .

"Bad break, bad break," Zuzu said, shaking her head. "So, how does it feel being upped by an amateur?" She stared directly into the camera. "For those of you who don't know, a mysterious supergirl named Donna jumped into the water yesterday at the Brazil qualifiers, and had a ride to remember." She turned back to Cassie. "Did you see it?"

"I did," Cassie said. "And I thought it took a lot of guts for her to dive in and show the world what she's made of—even if it didn't count for the qualifiers." She loosened her finger cross. That part was actually true. Danica might be slimy, but she was far from a wimp. *Unlike me?* Cassie wondered. *I wasn't always so scared all the time. At least, not in the water* . . . She didn't want to think about it. "By the way, that mysterious surfer's name isn't Donna. It's Danica. We're bunkmates here at Camp Ohana."

"Really? That's fantastic!" Zuzu said. "Maybe you can get us an interview? Hmm?"

Cassie glanced at Zuzu. "Maybe . . ."

. . . *Never?*

And that was when Cassie did it. She looked.

She saw Zeke and Haydee and the kids out there in the water. But Micah was gone. *Where'd he go?* Cassie wondered. Then she decided it was probably better that she didn't know. She turned her attention back to the interview.

"You're the best, Cassie," Zuzu was saying. "So. What's next for you?"

"For me? Ummm . . ." Apart from the *Surf Girl* photo shoot, Cassie had no clue what was next. Her recent past had been so topsy-turvy that even her present seemed like a big question mark.

She glanced back outside to find Micah back in the water again with the others, demonstrating perfect form as he brought in a sweet wave. Then he pretended to fall off his board: "Wh-wh-whhhhhhhoa!" And the kids rustled around him, laughing.

How could he laugh like that when Cassie was feeling a mess inside? But the truth was that she wanted to be out there, too, laughing along with him as if nothing had happened. But no matter how much she wanted to, Cassie couldn't do-over last night.

"Cassie?" Zuzu asked. "Your future?"

"Oh. Right," Cassie said and decided to go for the canned answer. "For the rest of the year I'm going to focus totally on surfing, of course."

The only problem? She had to forget about Micah first.

Eight

Micah didn't have to be a rocket scientist to know that it was *really* hard to forget about an old girlfriend when she was about to be photographed in a swimsuit for the cover of a major surfing magazine.

He thought he was doing pretty well by throwing himself into his C.I.T. duties. But the beginner's surf lesson had ended early due to rough waters and a strong undertow. The rest of the day's surfing was cancelled for the same reason. So Micah needed another distraction—quick—preferably *before* Cassie came out of that interview in the canteen.

He collected the last two remaining Camp Ohana surfboards on the beach and carried them up to the supplies hut by the pool. After he hosed down all the boards he planned to rinse out the wet suits, too, even though it was Danica's turn to do it. She'd disappeared shortly after the end of the lesson today, but Micah was more than willing to let it slide.

Today I'm Super C.I.T. who hoses out stuff and who doesn't think about Cassie, Micah said to himself. *Wait. I just did, didn't I? Okay, starting now, I'm not going to think about her. Crap. I did it again.*

Okay, starting . . . now.

He reached the door to the supplies hut, pushed it open, and flicked on the lights.

Charlie and Andi instantly sprang apart.

"Whoa!" At first Micah was stunned. Then he smiled. *Charlie and Andi making out in the supply hut? No way!*

"Oh. Hey, Micah," Charlie said, suddenly pretending to count a heap of life jackets on a shelf. "We were just in here doing inventory."

In the dark? Micah thought.

"Yeah," Andi said, turning to the oars on the opposite wall. "There's a lot of stuff in here to count. One, two, three, four, five . . ."

"Riiiiight." Micah grinned wider. "You wouldn't mind cleaning all this stuff for me before you count it, would you?" He pointed to the wet suits and boards

157

piled up just outside the hut. Forget Super C.I.T. They needed some privacy.

"Oh, sure. Absolutely. No problem," Charlie said. He exchanged a glance with Andi and she nodded.

"Uh-huh. No problem at all," Andi added. "Thanks!"

"Thanks?" Micah asked. "For what?" He couldn't resist teasing them a little.

"Um." Andi seemed nervous.

"Uh, just for being you. Bye!" Charlie replied, then closed the door.

"Twenty-six, twenty-seven, twenty-eight . . ." Andi counted from inside. "Think he's gone yet?" she whispered.

Micah laughed. *Good for them*, he thought. And then . . . he wondered if Cassie knew. Because if she didn't he wanted to be the one to tell her. But of course he *couldn't* because of the things he'd told her last night.

Micah wasn't a fan of being honest with himself lately. If he were, he'd have already admitted that he might have kinda sorta overreacted to Cassie saying he wasn't a real surfer. That maybe he kinda sorta

158

knew deep down that she had no idea she'd struck a sore nerve with her words. That he kinda sorta wished he hadn't blown up at her.

Stupid mouth, Micah thought.

He knew he *wanted* to talk to Cassie about it, but he felt so foolish—and afraid that she might be the one to burn *him* this time.

A crowd seemed to suddenly swarm the pool area—photographers, a cameraman, assistants, and kids trying to catch a glimpse of what was going on. He even saw Danica and Ben taking in the scene.

In the center of it all was Cassie.

A woman with curly brown hair was talking to her. "Okay, Cassie. Just act naturally as we stroll to the beach." Then she yelled, "Would *some*body give her a surfboard! Do I have to do everything?"

An assistant quickly handed Cassie a white Coco Beach board, then pulled back into the crowd. "Sorry, Zuzu."

"Okay, we're chatting . . . we're chatting. Don't look at the video camera!" Zuzu told Cassie as they walked.

Micah tried to catch Cassie's eye. Just when he thought he had, a photographer bumped him out of the way, almost knocking him into the pool. "Dude!"

"Sorry, bro," the guy said, but kept clicking his camera as he shuffled backward.

Soon Cassie and the rest of the swarm were passing him by.

On impulse, Micah called out to her. "Cass!"

If she looks over, it means she wants to talk to me, too. Right?

Cassie thought she heard Micah call her name above the noise of the crowd. She tried to find him, but her *entourage* was practically pushing her toward the beach.

It couldn't be him, she decided, even though she *wanted* it to be him. Micah was probably still surfing with the beginner students, wasn't he?

"Give us a pose over here by the banyan tree, Cassie!" the photographer told her.

Cassie smiled as he took the shot; half the other people in the crowd took the shot, too. This was getting out of hand. She was beginning to feel like a circus freak.

Now Cassie was wishing she had asked Kiera to come to the shoot. As it was, Mr. Hainsbro was lurking in the background somewhere, probably still frowning even after she'd managed to mention Coco Beach *three times* in her interview. It was overkill, Cassie knew, but she wanted to make sure the sponsor was happy, though it looked as if that wasn't going to happen today.

Finally, Cassie was ushered to a spot near the water. A stylist twisted her hair into two braids and retouched her makeup. Zuzu came over to inspect the stylist's work. "Beautiful," she told Cassie. "Okay, Rafe. She's good to go!"

The photographer approached Cassie. "We're looking for a fresh and friendly vibe. We'll shoot a roll on the beach first, then maybe we'll get you in the water. Ready?"

Cassie planted the Coco Beach surfboard in the sand and nodded. "Let's do it," she said and struck her first pose.

Rafe clicked frame after frame, directing Cassie into different positions. After about ten minutes of shooting, Cassie heard Zuzu call out, "Hold it! Stop for a sec."

Rafe put down his camera. "What's the problem?"

"I don't know. It just doesn't feel . . . *spicy* enough," Zuzu said, shaking her head.

"Spicy?" Cassie placed a hand on her hip. "I thought you wanted fresh and friendly?"

Zuzu frowned. "Yes. Well, spice is always *implied*. Isn't that right, Rafe?"

"Absolutely." Rafe nodded. "Spice is a given. On *any* cover."

"So what can we do to give it some umph?" Zuzu asked.

"A better location? Add a guy to the scene?" Rafe suggested.

A different model? Cassie thought wryly, eyeing the semicircle of people that had gathered around the shoot. She secretly hoped to see Micah somewhere and was disappointed when she didn't. Instead, she spotted Simona and some girls from her swimming classes. Andi and Charlie were there; she gave them a little wave. Sasha, Sierra, and Ben were there, too. Danica was front and center, naturally . . . But Tori was a no-show, which was kind of irritating. Tori said she'd be there. So where was she?

"No," Zuzu was saying absently as she scanned the beach. "We need something . . ." Her voice trailed off as she grabbed Rafe by the shoulder and squeezed hard.

"Ow! Watch it, Zuzu!"

"I just came up with a brilliant idea!" Zuzu cried. She marched toward the crowd that had gathered around the shoot. "You!" she called. "I know you. You're that mystery girl from yesterday!"

Cassie's stomach dropped when she saw Zuzu pull a beaming Danica from her spot in the front row.

"We're going to retool the feature. Get her into makeup," Zuzu ordered the stylist. "And make sure she's in a Coco Beach swimsuit!" she added after a brief conference with Mr. Hainsbro.

About fifteen minutes later, Danica stepped onto the set with a hairstyle identical to Cassie's and wearing a teeny cinnamon-colored bikini that was sure to add spice to the cover.

Cassie glared at the girl, suddenly feeling like a grandma in her sporty one-piece. "You planned this," she murmured through gritted teeth.

"I didn't, I *swear*," Danica said.

Cassie narrowed her eyes. "Right. Just like you came to the qualifiers yesterday for *moral support*?"

"Okay, you have a point, but I'm telling the truth about this. I could never have planned something so perfect. And even if I had, do you think I'd keep it a secret?" Danica asked. "Oh, and now that I'm here? You'd better bring it, because you know *I* will."

"We'll see who brings it," Cassie said. She thought she heard Danica mutter "Finally" but she wasn't sure.

"Okay, ladies. Get into the water about yea high," Rafe said, indicating mid-calf.

Cassie and Danica entered, but it wasn't easy to stay put. The surf was unusually rough.

Rafe rolled up his pants and followed them in taking his camera. "Look like you're having fun together," he said and started shooting.

Danica splashed in the water as she smiled at the camera, then at Cassie, as if they were best friends. Cassie tried to do the same, but was having a hard time looking spicy with the surfboard under her arm. She tried to plant it upright but was knocked off balance by a rogue wave.

"Ahh!" She tripped over the board and fell into the water.

Then she started to laugh. Not one of those cute modely laughs—a gigantic belly guffaw that started to hurt her stomach after a minute.

Danica was laughing, too.

"Oh, you think it's funny, Danica?" Cassie asked, still sitting in the shallows. She lunged out her foot and tripped her. Danica fell into the water next to Cassie, a tiny piece of seaweed clinging onto her cheek.

The two girls laughed even harder.

"Perfect!" Dan shouted. "Give me more."

Cassie splashed Danica but stopped when she thought she heard something. *Was that a scream?*

"What is it?" Danica asked.

"Wait. *Shh.*" Cassie listened harder for it, but nothing. She was about to give up when she heard it again—a faint cry for help! Cassie sprang to her feet. "I think someone's in trouble." She turned her head to inspect the beach. Everything seemed fine there. She squinted out to sea, shading her eyes with her hand.

Nothing but waves . . .

Then a head and pair of arms suddenly bobbed out above the breakers. They appeared for only a few seconds before they disappeared.

"There!" Cassie cried, pointing. "Someone's out there! Where's the lifeguard?" She leaped out of the water with the surfboard under her arm and raced down the beach, full force.

Danica was not far behind, and the onlookers followed her.

When Cassie reached the point where she thought she'd seen the swimmer, she stopped, panting as she searched the ocean for another sign. *"There!"* she pointed way out in the distance. It was a girl, flailing her arms above her head!

Cassie's eyes darted to the red flags flapping in the breeze. *No wonder there's no lifeguard—no one's supposed to be in the water!*

Then she caught sight of something even more horrifying. Her lemon-colored surfboard, cracked in two, was getting tossed between the waves! Her heart stopped when she made the connection.

"Tori!" Cassie screamed. Instinctively she sprinted into the water, grasping her Coco Beach board from the photo shoot.

"Wait! Cassie! Don't go!" she heard Danica yell. "I see sharks! Seriously! I'm not kidding!"

Sharks? Cassie froze in place. Her pulse raced as her body trembled with fear. No, she couldn't let that stop her. How could she?

It's Tori out there. I have to save her!

Cassie chucked her board into the water, hopped on, and immediately began to paddle hard. Breakers splashed her face as her arms pounded the surf. Cassie held her breath and duck-dived her board underneath a large oncoming wave. When she surfaced she found that she was almost there.

Tori thrashed about, trying to stay afloat, as the unforgiving sea pummeled her body. "Cass! . . . Hellll—" she cried before going under.

"No!" Cassie's arms burned as she drove her board forward. Then she reached into the dark waters, searching for an arm, a leg—anything she could grab hold of. Her hand skimmed the nape of Tori's wet suit and Cassie pulled. She pulled with all her force. With strength she didn't know possible, she pulled her cousin to the surface.

Exhausted, Tori coughed and sputtered, and Cassie forgot all about the threat of sharks as she dove into the deep to hold her cousin above water. When she was sure Tori was ready, Cassie propped her onto the surfboard and held her securely so she wouldn't fall off.

"Cass—"

"You're okay now. I've got you," Cassie said.

Tori nodded, and relaxed her head on the board for a moment. When she lifted it back up, her face grew pale. Her mouth opened but she couldn't utter any words.

"Tori, what is it?" Cassie asked. Then, when she heard the rumble, she knew. She turned her head just in time to see the monster swell rushing toward them. "Oh, God!" Cassie cried and jumped onto the surfboard behind her cousin. "Hold on, Tori, as tight as you can! You hear me?"

Tori pulled her body into a ball, clutching the surfboard so firmly, her knuckles turned white. And Cassie leaned over her, trying to paddle toward shore. She had to get more speed!

Soon she felt the wave take them into its hollow. This was it. Cassie popped up to her feet, trying to center their weight on the surfboard. She prayed that they wouldn't wipe out.

Somehow, the board stayed solid. They flew across the water's surface, cutting through the frothy waters as Cassie carried them home to shore.

When the girls reached the shallows, Cassie helped her winded cousin out of the water.

Tori collapsed onto the sand. "You rode that wave . . . you conquered your fear . . . you saved my life!" she said between breaths, before the throng gathered around them.

Cassie kneeled next to her. "I guess I did."

But in her heart she knew only one thing mattered.

Tori was safe.

Nine

"They made it!" Danica said to Ben, even though it was kind of obvious. She couldn't take her eyes off Cassie as people congratulated the heroine over and over, clapping and patting her on the back for a job well done.

Of course, Danica would have done the same thing if she'd had a surfboard . . . *and* if she hadn't seen those shark fins circling in the ocean. Danica was adventurous, but she wasn't *crazy*. Which was why she was totally speechless at the moment. Wasn't Cassie afraid to go in the water *because* of the sharks?

"You were absolutely brilliant, Cassie!" Zuzu said, exposing her set of perfectly capped teeth. "We got the whole rescue on video *and* on film. It's an amazing story." She turned to Tori. "And how's our girl?"

"I'm okay . . . just a little shaken up, I guess," Tori said as the camp nurse checked her out on the beach.

"What were you doing out there, Tori?" Simona asked. "Didn't you see the red flags? It means the water is too rough."

"I wanted to practice my surfing for a little while," Tori said sheepishly. "I thought I could handle it."

"You're a beginner and you *thought you could handle it*?" Danica had to speak up. She was glad that Tori was okay, but nothing bugged her more than someone who didn't respect the power of the ocean. Okay, there were a few things that bugged her more, but this was serious. "We saw *sharks* out there, Tori, but I suppose you thought you could handle them, too."

"Sharks?" Tori looked at Cassie and gulped. "Really?"

Cassie nodded. "Danica spotted them just before I went in for you."

"Danica, about those sharks . . ." Simona was examining the horizon with a pair of binoculars. "Looks like they're a family of dolphins."

A few kids laughed and Danica felt her cheeks flush. "No way," she said, squinting to find the dorsal fins in the water again. "I know what I saw."

"Take a closer look." Simona handed Danica the binoculars.

Danica put the binoculars to her eyes. Sure enough, she saw three dolphins surfacing then dipping back into the ocean. "I don't believe it."

"Let me see." Ben took the binoculars and put them to his eyes. "Yup. Dolphins. But they're *very* sinister-looking," he said. "It's an honest mistake."

"Thanks, Ben," Danica whispered, but she was still embarrassed.

"Well, I think we've all had enough excitement for the day," Simona said. "Let's pack it in."

"Actually . . ." Zuzu said, "we were right in the middle of our photo shoot. Is it okay if we finish it?"

Simona looked at Cassie, then at Danica. "It's up to the girls."

"It's fine with me," Danica said.

"Ah, yes . . . that's wonderful," Zuzu said, fixing her glasses. "But since the theme of our feature has changed significantly, we need to tweak the cover.

So . . . you're out." She turned to Tori. "And *you're* in. How would you like to be a Surf Girl?"

"Me?" Tori's pale skin appeared to brighten. "Like, on the cover and everything?"

Simona shook her head. "I'm not so sure Tori is up—"

"I'll do it, Zuzu!" Tori cried. Suddenly energized, she leaped to her feet and struck a pose. "I am so ready. And I know exactly what bathing suit I want to wear." She nudged Cassie. "So, can I borrow it?"

"You can *have* it." Cassie laughed and linked arms with her cousin. "Come on. Let's do this."

"But . . ." Danica watched Cassie lead the gaggle of campers and counselors down the beach as if she were some kind of Pied Piper. Even Sasha and Sierra were following at the back of the pack, all chatty and giggly and totally forgetting about Danica.

Don't I deserve to be on the cover of a surfing magazine, too? Danica was glad that Tori had come through okay. Of *course* she was. But after all the early mornings, all that work on her board, the awesome showing at the qualifiers yesterday . . .

Ben put an arm around her shoulders. "You got robbed."

"I know," Danica replied, trying to shake off the disappointment. "Whatever. I never liked that rag, anyway."

Later that evening, after the photo shoot was over and the excitement had died down, Cassie and Tori hung out alone in Tori's bunk.

"What a crazy day," Tori said, leaning back into the pillows on her bed.

"Tell me about it," Cassie agreed. "You had me scared there for a minute."

"I had myself scared," Tori admitted. "Have I thanked you for saving my butt yet?"

"Only about twenty times," Cassie said. "I know you would have done the same for me."

Tori nodded. "In a heartbeat." Then she winced. "Um, did I tell you how sorry I am for wrecking your new surfboard? I am *so* lame. Sorry, Cass."

"Forget it," Cassie said with a wave of a hand. "It was a freebie from Coco Beach and the color was sort of on the obnoxious side. And anyway, you're not lame," she added. "If anyone's lame here it's me."

Tori gave Cassie a look that said *You've got to be kidding me.* "How are *you* lame?"

Cassie didn't want to get into it. Now wasn't the time to be complaining about her lack of social graces when it came to boys. It seemed so silly after what happened to Tori. "Never mind. Let's just drop it."

"*Tell* me, Cass." Tori grabbed Cassie's hand. "Come on."

Cassie was silent.

"Is it Micah?" Tori asked gently. "Did you talk to him yet?"

Cassie shook her head. "What would I say?" She tried to swallow the lump in her throat. "He was my first real boyfriend and I blew it. I want him back, but I don't know what to do. I guess me and my big mouth will be very happy together."

"Oh, Cass . . ."

"You want to hear something weird?" Cassie went on. "I miss him so much, I thought I heard him calling my name today. Talk about delusional . . . and *lame.*"

"You want to talk lame? How about almost drowning in front of your crush—*twice*?" Tori said. She waved. "Hello, *lame*-o!"

"You mean when you faked a wipeout a couple of weeks ago so our little surfer, Lance, would notice you?" Cassie remembered it well. She'd been so worried about Tori, then so upset when she'd found out the truth.

"Okay, okay." Tori held up her hands in defense. "The first time was a totally despicable ploy to feel Lance's muscles," she said. "But *he* doesn't know that. As far as Lance is concerned, I'm a big fat airhead who should forget riding waves and stick to sunbathing and fashion magazines."

"Tori! You sound as if you actually *like* surfing." Cassie felt a certain amount of pride in that.

"Well, duh!" Tori said. "I guess it kind of grew on me."

Someone knocked at the screen door. A moment later it cracked open and Lance popped his head in. "You guys decent?" he asked with a grin.

"Come join the party," Tori said, waving him inside.

Lance entered the bunk. He had one arm behind his back as if he were hiding something. "So, I got you a little get-well present," he said.

"Really?" Tori did a little happy clap. "I love presents! What is it?"

"Say hello to . . . Mr. Bunny!" Lance whipped out a floppy white stuffed rabbit from behind his back and handed it to Tori.

"Aw, he's so cute!" Tori cooed. "Where did you find him?"

"In the day-campers' cabin," Lance said proudly. "There are so many stuffed animals in that bunk, the kid'll probably never miss it."

Tori tilted her head. "Huh?"

This, Cassie thought, *is my cue to go.* "Well, I'm going to head back to my bunk. Kinda tired." She faked a yawn and headed out.

"Wait a sec." Tori got off her bed and joined her by the door. "Can I give you some advice about Micah?" she asked. "Or at least, a suggestion?"

Cassie nodded. "Okay."

"Well, I think there's only one way for you to figure this whole thing out," Tori said. "You have to do what you always used to do when you needed answers—before you got so caught up in, you know, *stuff*."

"Yeah. Thanks, Tori," Cassie said as if she

actually *understood* what her cousin was talking about. In truth, she had no clue.

But as she walked the path from Tori's bunk to her own, she could hear the sound of the waves breaking gently onto the beach—a rhythm almost calling to her—and suddenly Tori's words became clear. Cassie knew exactly what she needed to do.

Cassie found herself on the beach early the next morning, grasping her surfboard and staring out into the beautiful ocean. It had taken a while for her to get it, but once she had, she realized how right her cousin was.

Tori knew that in the past whenever Cassie had a problem—any problem—she always used to surf on it. Some people saw things clearly after they'd had a little sleep, but not Cassie. The soothing rock of the waves, the salt of the water, the adrenaline rush after a successful ride—Cassie wasn't sure what it was that freed her mind. What she *did* know was that in the end, without fail, she'd have an answer, a direction.

Somehow Cassie's problems always seemed to work themselves out after a good surf.

And then her life got hectic with traveling, training, competitions . . . there was barely enough time in the day to breathe, let alone to reflect. Then the shark attack happened . . . and the fear came. Surfing had suddenly *become* the problem.

But Cassie had spent enough time out of the water. So what was she waiting for?

Cassie ran for the ocean, surfboard in tow. She dived in without hesitation, letting the salt water engulf her. A few minutes later she was on her surfboard, paddling out to the deep. Even after months without training, Cassie felt good out there. Strong.

When she finally reached the place she wanted to be, she switched onto her back, letting the morning sun warm her face. She took in a deep breath, exhaled, and relaxed.

And as the ocean gently rocked her back and forth Cassie waited.

She waited for her inspiration . . . or the perfect swell.

Whichever came first.

Ten

"No way. She is *not* surfing here."

Cassie Hamilton was the absolute *last* person Danica wanted to see during her early-morning surf. But there she was, performing a perfect floater across the top of a small pealing wave.

For someone who called herself a pro surfer, Cassie seemed to lack any kind of surfing ethics. Danica had been doing dawn patrol at this spot all summer, *solo*, which was how Danica liked it. And Cassie knew it.

What? Did she just assume that I'd step aside and give her the best waves at Camp Ohana now that she's back in the water? Or maybe she's here to kick me off my primo spot.

"I don't think so." Danica wasn't about to let that happen, and she wasn't into sharing, either. She carried her board to the sea without even as much as a warm-up stretch. If Cassie wanted these waves, she would have to fight for them.

Maybe Danica would finally get to see what the girl was made of. She paddled out to the spot where Cassie was waiting on her board.

"Hey," Cassie said. "They're breaking right."

Danica rolled her eyes. "Oh, really? You mean like they've been doing all summer? I know this because I've been surfing here—*all summer.*"

"What's the matter with *you*?" Cassie asked. "Did you fall out of bed or something?"

"Yeah. That's it." Danica saw a wave approaching. She paddled for it, then rode it in. When she returned, Cassie was still sitting in the same spot.

"Nice," Cassie said.

"I don't need your commentary, thanks," Danica replied. "Maybe you should try surfing down the beach. It's a little crowded here, don't you think?"

Cassie shrugged. "Not really." She took the next wave and rode it in effortlessly.

The next one was Danica's. She shredded

through it as if she were on a mission—which she was. "Let's see you beat that," she said, when she'd paddled back to their little lineup.

"I thought we weren't *doing* commentary," Cassie replied, but she kept a casual vibe as she glided backside through her next ride.

She's not even trying to show me up, Danica thought. *So why is she even here? What's the point?*

"Way to shred it," she said sarcastically when Cassie had returned, hoping to squeeze a reaction out of the girl. *This is where we're finally going to get into it. Go head-to-head. May the best surfer win, right?*

But Cassie wasn't biting. Instead, she ignored Danica. Stretching her arms overhead, she closed her eyes and tilted her face toward the sun.

What is her problem? Danica huffed and took the next wave, determined to tear it up, which she did.

When Danica returned to the line, she saw a real swell forming in the distance. Up until then the surf had been on the small side—good for practicing cutbacks but nothing thrilling. She wished the wave was hers, but she wasn't about to drop in front of

182

Cassie—or was she? Maybe it would tick off Cassie enough to *do* something.

But then Cassie said, "Go for it," offering up the wave.

Which, in turn, ticked off *Danica*!

She stared at the girl. "Are you *insane*? You're giving me the best wave of the day so far? What do you think I am? Some charity case?"

"What are you talking about?" Cassie asked.

The two girls eyed each other as their boards lifted with the swell, then sank back down as the wave passed them by.

"I'm talking about *you*," Danica said. "You want to know what *I* think?" she went on. "I think you're afraid of a little *friendly* competition. Because you're afraid I'll win. I'm right, aren't I? You saw me kick it at the Brazil qualifiers and you got scared. Come on. Say it. 'Danica, you're—"

"Would you shut up already?!" Cassie cried. "God, Danica, I just want to surf! Not everything is a competition!"

Danica was stunned. First because she'd never heard Cassie raise her voice so loudly and second, her words made Danica think back to something that had been niggling at her brain for days.

She knew how good a surfer Cassie was. Cassie could have beaten those girls in the Honoli'i lineup with her eyes closed. So how come she freaked out during a simple surfing competition, yet she was able to dive in and save her cousin when she thought there were sharks in the water?

Something about it all just didn't sit right with Danica.

"You faked it," she blurted out. "You faked being sick at the Brazil qualifiers. You threw your game on purpose, didn't you?" It was all too clear now. Cassie must be seriously disturbed to want to ruin her career like that. And for what?

"No!" Cassie said instantly. "I would never do that. Why would I do that? I wouldn't!"

But Danica wasn't buying it. Cassie was denying it too strongly. "Are you sure about that, Cassie?"

"What? Am I sure? Of *course* I'm sure. I can't believe you would even *say* that." Cassie let her voice trail off as she stared at her surfboard. "I mean . . . I didn't throw the heat on purpose," she said. "I was seriously freaked, but, um . . ."

"Say it," Danica urged her.

"Every surfer has a certain amount of fear. It's healthy, but you have to push through it, right?" Cassie began. "But in Honoli'i, at the Brazil qualifiers . . . I didn't. I gave in to it—big-time. I guess you could say I gave up."

"You gave up?" Danica echoed. "Why?"

"I don't know. Maybe I didn't *want* it, you know?"

"No, I *don't*," Danica said.

"It's hard to explain." Cassie shrugged. She dipped her hands into the ocean and swirled them around, feeling the water push between her fingertips. Finally, she looked at Danica. "I used to have this hunger to compete, right? But then the shark thing happened and I just . . . *lost* it. Maybe I even lost it before the attack, I'm not sure," she added. "Or . . . maybe I didn't want to admit that sometimes the stress of being a pro surfer really rots. Maybe so many people put all this time and effort into building me up that I didn't want to disappoint them. Maybe I didn't realize it until today, when I put my board into the water for the first time without any pressure, that all this competing is totally sucking the joy out of surfing.

Maybe I took so long to get back on my board because I was afraid of sharks *and* going back to the pressure cooker." Cassie shook her head. "No. I don't think I want that anymore. Not enough, at least."

Danica was having a hard time processing. She didn't know what to say. For her, it was all about the competition, the dedication it took to work toward a goal—be it on surfboards or with boys. It was about the satisfaction when the work paid off and the determination to work harder when it didn't. It was about succeeding. How could Cassie not want all that?

"So what *do* you want?" Danica asked her.

"A normal life, I guess," Cassie replied. "A life that includes surfing, of course, but I want it to be on my *own* terms. I want to go to a regular school instead of being tutored on the road. I want to spend time with my family—not just my coach and handlers. I want to have good friends—*real* ones—not just the familiar faces I see at all the surfing events. I want a boyfriend . . ." She paused. "I *almost* had that. Unfortunately my big mouth messed it up. I said some stuff to Micah that I didn't mean and—" Cassie stopped again. "Why am I even telling you this?" she asked, more to herself than to Danica. "You know what? You win. You can have your surfing spot all to yourself. I'm out of here."

Cassie squinted at the horizon in the distance, searching for the next swell. Once she found it she turned her board and paddled hard until her fins had caught hold.

And Danica watched in silent awe as Cassie rode the wave to shore, not surprised by the girl's perfect form but shocked to realize that Cassie kind of wanted the life that Danica already had.

"But how do I know when to turn my board and start paddling for a wave?" Kenny asked Micah the next day. Kenny was a twelve-year-old newbie who couldn't quite catch a curl yet.

"Dude, it's all about timing," Micah explained. "Tell me this. Where do we want the wave to be when we pop up?"

"Underneath the board just as it's about to break?" Kenny asked.

"You got it." Micah nodded. "So, you've got to

watch the wave. See how it's forming. See how fast it's coming," he said. "Sometimes you have to paddle only a couple of strokes before the wave reaches you and you're in position to ride. But if it looks like the wave is going to break somewhere between you and the beach, then you've got to paddle your butt off if you want to catch that one. Got it?"

"I think so," Kenny said.

"Then what are you waiting for?" Micah pointed the boy toward the ocean. "Let me see you rip!"

"Yeah!" Kenny yelled as he ran for the surf.

Micah laughed as he watched Kenny charge the water. He wasn't sure if the kid would ride a curl today, but after enough time in the water he'd get a feel for it eventually.

Micah liked helping out the surfing classes. It was fun and a good distraction. He actually found himself *not* obsessing over a certain surfer girl for minutes at a time.

But then, at times like these, when he was watching the kids surf from the beach, he couldn't help thinking about her. He'd run through the scenario of their argument over and over in his brain.

Why did he open his mouth without thinking?

So what if she was a better surfer than he was? That didn't make Micah a *bad* surfer, and he was getting better with every set. So why did he let that one little comment bug him so much?

Because he let his pride get the better of him, that's why.

And now he felt stupid and jerky and too embarrassed to talk to her about it. Did he mention *stupid*?

Cassie probably wouldn't speak with him, anyway. She'd barely looked at him since their *stupid* fight. And Micah didn't blame her.

Gotta stop thinking about it, Micah told himself. *You're gonna drive yourself nuts!*

He turned his focus to the ocean in time to see Kenny *just miss* catching a curl. He cupped his mouth with his hands and yelled, "Almost had it, Kenny!"

Then he spotted an eleven-year-old named Abby who was surfing a decent sized wave with Danica. And she was doing great! She made a clean bottom turn on her long board. Then she started trimming the face of the wave!

This was the little girl who, not too long ago, was afraid to stand on a surfboard in the water.

Micah couldn't help remembering how Cassie had helped. She wouldn't let the frightened girl give up. He'd been impressed by how patient Cassie was with her, giving her pointers, telling her surfing stories. Eventually Abby overcame her fear—all because of Cassie.

And now Danica had taught Abby how to shred, which was also impressive.

Abby ended her run with a minor wipeout in the white water. Almost immediately she was pulling Danica to go back to the waves, but it was time to end the lesson.

Micah helped Zeke call the boys out of the water. Then he headed over to Danica, who was talking with Abby.

"Did you see me out there, Micah?" Abby asked.

"Uh-huh," Micah said. "You were awesome."

"I know!" Abby cried. "I've got to go call my sister. She's gonna freak when I tell her." She ran up the beach in her wet suit.

Micah turned to Danica. "You were pretty awesome, too," he said, patting her on the back. "With Abby, I mean."

"Micah, Micah, Micah . . ." Danica shook her head, clicking her tongue. "Please. Don't bother."

"Huh?" Micah was confused. "Don't bother what?"

Danica gave him a serious look. "Come on. *You* know and *I* know that you're still into me. And it's true, you may have gotten the wrong idea because I was such a *good friend* in your time of need . . ."

No way. She thinks I still like her as a girlfriend? "Hey, Danica. You've got it all wrong. I—"

Danica held up a hand to stop him. "Micah. I *said*, don't *bother*." She sighed, and shook her head. "I didn't want to have to do it this way, but you leave me no choice. I'm dumping you—*again*."

"You're dumping me." Micah almost laughed when he realized what she was doing. *She knows I don't like her like that anymore so she's trying to save face!* "Come on, Danica. You don't have to—"

"Look, there's nothing you can do to change my mind, okay?" Danica said, interrupting him. "I'm with Ben now. I'm sorry it had to come to this,

Micah. I hope this little issue doesn't come between our friendship," she said. Then she actually held out her hand for a shake.

Micah glanced at her hand. *She can't be serious.*

But clearly she was. So he shook it. "You broke my heart, Danica. But how could I stay mad at you," he said, keeping a straight face and going along with the game.

"Good," Danica said. "Besides, you and Cassie were both whining to me about each other, I couldn't stand it. If you ask me, you guys are a match made in whiny heaven. Anyway, I'm glad we had this little talk. See you around camp." She began to walk away.

"Wait a sec," Micah said, stopping her. "Cassie's been talking about me? What did she say?"

Danica rolled her eyes. "The usual. That she misses you, blah, blah, blah. In between sobbing her eyes out, of course," she said. "*So* annoying."

"She misses me?" Micah asked with a slight smile.

"Micah? Do you need a hearing aid?" Danica placed her hands on her hips. "Do me a favor. Would you please put yourselves out of this misery, and go kiss her already?" she said. "And leave me out of it!" She turned on her heel and stomped up the beach.

Gladly, Micah thought, watching her go. *But I can't just go up to Cassie and kiss her—not after all that was said.*

Can I?

"Okay, so get this," Tori told Cassie at dinner that evening. "Andi over here says that kissing Charlie is better than eating a double-dipped chocolate covered s'more. And I say that's totally impossible."

"It's not!" Andi countered. "Charlie's kisses are super sweet, just like the legendary s'more, only with*out* the calories. Get it?"

"But," Tori added. "There's nothing on the face of this planet *better* than a s'more. What do you think, Cassie?"

"I think we have to get Charlie over here so we can settle this, right now," Cassie replied. "Ooh. There he is! Tori, you can kiss him first to find out." She raised her hand to flag him over. "Charlie!"

Andi pulled on Cassie's arm. "Stop!" she said, giggling. "Cut it out!"

Cassie laughed. "What?" she asked innocently. "I'm just saying . . ."

Tori was laughing, too, but then her face dropped.

"What's the matter?" Cassie asked her.

"Ugh." Tori nodded in the direction of the salad bar. "Little Miss *Sunshine* is on her way over here," she said. "And my question is, *why*?"

Cassie glanced over her shoulder. Sure enough Danica was crossing the canteen, carrying a tray with a huge salad and a bottle of water. "Don't worry about it," she said. "It's cool."

Danica approached the table, but it wasn't as if she was staying. She didn't put down her tray.

"Well?" Cassie asked her.

"It's all set," Danica replied.

"What is?" Tori asked, looking from Cassie to Danica.

But Danica ignored her. "He knows that you still like him," she told Cassie. "He'll get back together with you in no time. He just needed the added reassurance."

194

"Who?" Andi asked. "Micah? Cassie! Tell me you guys are getting back together!"

"Or at least tell us what's going on," Tori added.

Cassie took a sip of her cherry punch and set it back down on the table. "Well, Danica had a little chat with Micah during the beginners' surfing session today and she let it slip that I miss him—accidentally on purpose, of course. She thinks that's all he needed to hear to make the first move. I would do it but . . ." She paused. "Oh, who am I kidding? I wouldn't do it. I feel too dumb. I know I'm being such a wuss about this, but I can't help it."

Cassie had fantasized about walking up to Micah, kissing him on the lips, and telling him that life was too short for silly arguments. But, no matter how much she wanted to, she knew she could never bring herself to go through with it. So, yesterday, when Danica returned from her early-morning surf session and offered to help Cassie get back together with Micah . . . well, Cassie knew she had to take her up on it.

Cassie turned back to Danica. "Are you sure this is going to work? 'Cause if you're wrong, I might lose Micah forever."

"Oh, it'll work, all right," Tori chimed in. "Case in point: Last night I had my bunkmate Jessica talk to Eddie and put it in his brain that *he* wanted to get back together with *me*. And *that* worked."

Andi tilted her head. "Tori? Are you sure you're fourteen?"

"Wait. Rewind," Cassie said, confused. "Last I knew you were with Lance. What happened to *him*?"

"Oh, please." Tori rolled her eyes. "Do you really think that I'd go out with a guy who steals stuffed animals from innocent little children? Even if it was for me? A girl's got to have standards, right?"

Cassie noticed that a short boy with shaggy hair was hovering by their table. "Uh, Tori?" he asked. "Lance wanted me to tell you that he gave back the bunny. He's waiting for you over there." The boy pointed across the room.

"Oh. Really," Tori said, sounding bored. She casually glanced over there, as did the rest of the table, to find Lance standing by the soda fountains holding a beautiful purple orchid. "Okay. Thanks for the message," she told the boy. As soon as he left, Tori smiled brightly. "Sometimes a girl's got to be forgiving, too, right?" she said. "See you guys later!"

"Or not!" Cassie called.

"Yeah. And *sometimes* a girl's got to go get dessert." Andi pulled back her seat and stood.

"S'mores?" Cassie asked with a sly smile.

"*No,*" Andi replied. "They're serving strawberry shortcake. Want some?"

"Sure," Cassie told her.

Once they were alone, Danica put down her tray and sat across from Cassie. "So, I did my part," she said. "*Now* will you speak to Kiera for me?"

Right. Danica wouldn't just go and talk to Micah out of the goodness of her heart. She'd made Cassie swear on her new surfboard that she'd help Danica go pro in return. "I already told you that I would—whether you helped me or not," Cassie reminded her. "Kiera said she'd hook you up with a surfing coach she knows in south Florida . . . but only if your parents are on board."

"Oh, I assure you, they'll be cool with it. I'll make sure of that." Danica clasped her hands. "Oh my God. I'm so psyched, I could kiss you!" she cried. "But I won't."

"Hey, I'm glad I could help you out," Cassie said. It was weird being friendly with her.

Danica narrowed her eyes. "Oh, and just so we're clear? Don't even *think* about holding this over my head," she said. "As far as I'm concerned, I did my part, so I don't owe you a thing."

"Fine," Cassie replied. *Ah, well. So much for friendly.* She figured their truce wouldn't last long. But it wasn't something she'd lose sleep over. Danica was so focused on being number one. Cassie wasn't sure if Danica knew how to be nice to *anybody*.

But one thing was certain. She'd make a heck of a pro surfer!

Eleven

"*She misses you . . .*" Micah couldn't get Danica's words out of his head. All day he'd been thinking about them, about Cassie.

Because he missed her, too.

He couldn't help wondering, though, if Danica was playing with him this morning. She was known to pull a good prank, but even Danica wasn't *that* heartless. She couldn't be. Right?

Only one way to find out, Micah had thought.

Finally, he'd worked up the nerve to talk to Cassie. But what would he say? He crossed the camp, planning out different starts to the conversation. *Hi, I know I've been a jerk but . . . Hey, Danica told me you miss me . . . Cassie, can we talk?*

None of it seemed right, but Micah wasn't too worried about it. He knew that as soon as he saw her, the words would come. And if they didn't, then maybe he'd do what Danica had suggested. Maybe he'd take Cassie in his arms and just kiss her.

He'd give anything to be able to kiss her again.

Finally Micah had reached Cassie's bunk. He climbed the steps to the lanai just as the door was opening. *Cassie?* he hoped. But no, it was Sasha and Sierra.

"Is Cassie in there?" he asked them, nodding toward the cabin.

"Nope." Sierra shook her head.

"I think she's at dinner," Sasha added.

"Thanks." Micah turned on his heel and headed for the mess hall. "Catch you guys later."

The closer he came to the canteen, the faster his heart began to pump. When he reached the entrance he stopped to take a deep breath before he entered, though it didn't do much good. He could practically hear his heartbeat thudding as he searched the tables for Cassie's face.

He saw her almost instantly. She was sitting at a middle picnic table with Tori, Andi, Charlie, and Danica, of all people. Cassie was doubled over and laughing at something Tori had just told her. She looked fresh and pretty with her hair pulled back into a ponytail and not at all as if she'd been crying her eyes out over him.

Micah swallowed hard. He was determined to talk to Cassie anyway, and started for her table.

"Hey! We haven't seen you in *sooo* long!" Sasha said as she and Sierra passed him by, then went to join Cassie and the rest of the group.

Micah's hands began to sweat. *How am I supposed to pour my heart out to Cassie in front of all those people?* he wondered.

The thing was, he couldn't. The conversation they needed to have was most definitely a private one. He slowed his pace, trying to catch Cassie's eye. *Come on, look up*, he silently urged her. *Look at me . . .*

And then, as if by magic, she did! Micah smiled slightly at Cassie, praying for a positive reaction. She trailed him with her eyes as he crossed the room then exited the mess hall. He hoped that she'd stand up, say *later* to her friends, and follow him outside. So he waited for her by the door.

After a few minutes Micah peeked back into the mess hall to find Cassie chatting busily with her friends, most likely about him. *She's not coming*, he realized.

Okay, so maybe his walking through the mess hall didn't exactly say, *Follow me, Cassie. We need to talk.* But Micah was *not* about to go back in there for a replay. And maybe it wasn't the right approach, either. Then what was?

Micah headed around the back of the canteen and briskly walked the path toward his cabin to think it through. He slowed his pace as he approached Cassie's bunk and eventually came to a stop.

Should I just wait for her here? he wondered, then decided against it. *Too stalkerish. Plus, she'll probably come back with most of the dinner crew.* Then he had an idea. *Maybe I could ask her to meet me somewhere.*

Yes, that was it. He'd write her a note.

Since no one was inside Cassie's bunk, Micah bound up the steps and onto the lanai. He pushed the door open and entered the cabin.

He spotted a pad of blue notepaper and a pen resting on Andi's nightstand. Micah picked them up and scribbled Cassie a note:

Cassie,

Meet me at the end of the pier at 9:00. Let's talk, okay?

He tapped the pen to his lips, thinking. Then he added:

I miss you.
—Micah

Micah read over the note. It was short but it said exactly what he wanted to say. He decided he was happy with it, then placed the paper facedown on Cassie's pillow.

A moment later, Micah thought he heard a group of chatty voices coming toward the cabin and his pulse quickened. *They're back already?* He quickly crossed to the window to peek outside. *No, just a bunch of counselors joking around.* They passed by Cassie's bunk without so much as a glance.

Micah was relieved, but maybe it was time to go. He glanced at his note resting safely on Cassie's pillow. Then he hurried to the door, opened it, and swiftly pulled it closed, hoping that Cassie would choose to see him tonight.

He had no idea that the force of the door had created a breeze. He did not see Cassie's note float into the air. Nor did he see it gently flutter back down, skimming the side of Cassie's pillow and slipping silently into the shadows underneath her bed.

"Oh my God!" Andi cried several days later. "Look what I found lurking underneath my bed!" She pulled out a dirty plastic blue snorkel and held it up. "I've been searching for this all summer and it's been here all along, hanging out with the dust bunnies." She brushed it off and chucked it on the top of her enormous open duffel bag, then struggled to zip the bag closed. "You almost ready, Cassie?"

"I have a few more things to pack and then I think I'll be done," Cassie said, checking around and playing with the pink-and-yellow friendship bracelet that Andi had given her a while back. "Oh, before I forget." She reached into the front pocket of her backpack and pulled out a necklace made of tiny shells that she had strung together in the craft hut. "I want you to have this," she said, handing it over.

"Oh, it's so beautiful!" Andi clasped the jewelry around her neck and gave Cassie a hug. "I love it. Thank you!"

Cassie held up her wrist, showing Andi the friendship bracelet. "I love my gift, too." She sighed and flopped onto her linen-stripped bed. "I still can't believe camp is over. It went so fast."

"Tell me about it," Andi said. "Charlie and I couldn't even talk about it last night. You don't know how much it costs to fly from Minnesota to New Mexico, do you?"

Cassie shook her head. "Sorry."

"Oh. Well, a long-distance thing will be tough, but we'll work it out," Andi said, but she didn't sound so confident. "I guess I should go spend some quality time with Charlie over by the airport buses. Meet you there?" She lugged her bag onto her shoulder.

"See you in a few," Cassie said, opening the door for Andi.

Long-distance relationships stink, Cassie thought. *Not that I'm an expert on relationships— at all.*

She tried not to think about Micah, but his face popped into her mind. She'd struggled to sort out what happened again and again but she still didn't understand it. When she'd seen Micah that evening smiling at her in the mess hall, she'd been shocked—and thrilled, of course. Everybody at the table had seemed psyched for her. Even Danica seemed cool with it, saying that she'd bet money that Cassie would find Micah waiting for her on the steps of their bunk.

But when they'd arrived back at the cabin, Micah wasn't there. In fact, he'd made himself pretty much scarce for the last days of camp. Cassie knew it was because he was avoiding her.

Why? she wondered. *He smiled at me. Didn't that mean he wanted to take the first step and ask me to talk? How come he never did?*

The tougher question Cassie had swirling around her brain was, *Then why didn't* you *take the first step? Why didn't you just go up and talk to him or kiss him or . . .* something*! What was stopping you?*

Cassie didn't have to search hard for the answer. She knew what was going on. She was scared. So she gave up on him rather than face her fear. Just as she'd almost given up on surfing.

As Cassie shoved the last few tops into her backpack she made a vow. *No more giving up*, she thought. *If I want something, I'm going to go for it until I get it.* If there was one thing she could take away from meeting Danica, it was that.

Cassie zipped her backpack closed and heaved it onto her shoulder. She took one more look around at the empty cabin. It was weird. After all the drama, she was really going to miss this place.

She turned and exited through the doorway and stepped out onto the lanai. She stopped to take in the hectic scene of kids and counselors lugging their stuff down the paths, only now it was toward the buses and not to their cabins. As Cassie started down the steps to join them, she felt as if she were forgetting something—because she *was*.

"Oh! My surfboard!"

She ran back up the steps, plopped her bag on the lanai, and entered the cabin again. Her new white Coco Beach board, which Mr. Hainsbro had so generously offered her after her yellow one had broken, was peeking out from underneath her bed.

Cassie grasped two of the fins and slid the board out. When she did, she noticed that something else came out along with it—a dusty piece of blue paper, probably from her notepad. She picked it up and almost crumpled it into a ball, when she noticed some writing. She read it—and gasped.

What Cassie was holding wasn't a simple scrap of notepaper. It was an actual *note*—from Micah! Asking her to meet him at the pier! Because he wanted to talk! Because he *missed* her!

Oh my God. He probably thinks I blew him off. That's why he's been avoiding me! Cassie realized. *When did he write this? Why didn't I see it? How could this have happened?* she wondered.

But none of it mattered. Still clutching the note, Cassie rushed outside and ran across the camp, straight to Micah's bunk. She flung the door open only to find it empty.

No! I'm too late! Cassie cried silently, her shoulders slumped as she leaned against the doorframe.

A moment later she heard a crackling noise, then Simona's voice was broadcasting over the Ohana sound system. "Okay, kids and counselors.

The buses are leaving in fifteen minutes. Please bring your bags to the parking lot if you haven't already done so. Thank you for another awesome summer. See you next year!"

Cassie slinked down the steps and back to her own cabin to pick up her things. It was time to go. What else could she do?

She went to the parking lot along with everybody else, hoping to see him there, but she couldn't find him. And now everybody was saying his and her good-byes and Cassie realized it was time for her to say good-bye, too.

She found Sierra and Sasha, then Charlie and Haydee and Zeke. She even gave Danica a hug.

"Cassie! Over here!" Tori cried, waving her over to the yellow school bus where Lance was trying to jam her three huge Louis Vuitton bags into the luggage bay. "I thought you weren't going to make it," she said, giving her a hug. "Is your brother picking you up?"

"Nah," Cassie said. "Home's not too far from the airport, so Simona arranged for me to get dropped off."

Just then a Camp Ohana cheer erupted among

the campers. Cassie and Tori joined right in, pumping their fists and chanting with ferocious enthusiasm, "*O* to the *H* to the *A* to the *Naaaaa*! *O* to the *H* to the *A* to the *Naaaaa*! *Aloha-lo-ha, Oha-naaaaa! Lo-ha-lo-ha, Oha-naaaaaaaaaaa!*"

It was funny. When she'd first heard that chant she'd thought it sounded like something from a cult revival, but now as she turned back to her cousin, she had tears in her eyes. "It can't be over, Tori. We were really getting to know each other. I'm gonna miss you so much!"

"Me too!" Tori cried, squeezing her tightly. They pulled apart and swiped at each other's tears, laughing and crying at the same time. "Don't worry," Tori told her. "I'm going to IM you so much you're going to want to block me."

"You promise?" Cassie asked.

Tori nodded. "Totally," she said. "So . . . what about Micah?" she whispered. "Have you seen him?"

Cassie shook her head. She didn't have the heart to explain about the note.

"Then find *him*," Tori said. "At least say good-bye."

"I tried," Cassie admitted. "He's already gone. Micah only lives up the coast in South Kohala. Somewhere in Waikui. He probably got a ride home." Cassie placed her backpack and her surfboard in the luggage bay. "I guess it just wasn't meant to be."

It was so heartbreaking. They'd be living so close to each other, they could go to homecoming together if they wanted to—if they were together.

Tori and Lance climbed the steps into the bus. Cassie was about to follow when she heard someone call her name. She turned to see Kiera hurrying toward her and waving.

"Hey! I came to give you a ride home," Kiera said. "My flight leaves at one, so I don't have to get the truck back to the rental place for another hour." She shrugged. "Guess the vacation's over."

Tori grasped Cassie's hand. "No, Cass, *pleeeeease* ride with us," she begged. "Every last minute counts. Who knows when we'll see each other again?"

This was true. "Thanks, Kiera, but I'm going to ride with my cousin," Cassie said.

"Okay," Kiera replied, "but, um . . ." She leaned in closer. "I also wanted to talk. You're sure you want

211

to take the rest of the year off, right? No Brazil, no Australia, no Japan?"

Cassie nodded. "I'm sure," she said. "I'm going to attend a real school for a change, make some real friends, and live a real regular life. And who knows, maybe I'll miss professional surfing and come back to it again."

"I understand." Kiera nodded. "But don't forget to call me when you're ready."

"I have a feeling that'll be around the end of June." Cassie smiled and hugged her coach. Even though Kiera was tough, Cassie was going to miss her, too. "Thanks for everything, Kiera," she said. "And thanks for being so cool about this."

"Take care of yourself. And don't forget to *call* me!" she said, backing away. She extended the thumb and pinky on her right hand and shook it, shooting Cassie the hang-loose sign.

Cassie waved good-bye to her coach, who turned and headed over to the next bus to speak to Danica. She sighed. This was it. Cassie was going home. She was getting everything she said she wanted—well, except for one thing.

"Thanks for the ride," Cassie told the driver,

and gave him her address. Then she made her way to the back of the bus—to the double seat next to Lance and Tori.

"Can you believe we'll be back in L.A. in mere hours?" Lance said to Tori.

Cassie glanced at her cousin, who gleamed as Lance held her hand. *Looks like Tori picked the right guy*, she thought. Cassie was happy for Tori. At least things worked out for one of them.

The bus hissed and the driver closed the door. He began to pull away but then jerked to a stop. A minute later the doors to the bus opened again.

Someone else was getting on. Cassie strained her neck to see . . .

Micah? Cassie realized, a smile curling onto her lips. *Yes! I was wrong! He* didn't *leave yet!*

But her smile faded when she saw that he wasn't so happy to see her. She watched him search the entire bus for an empty seat—until he realized that the only one available was next to her.

"Hi," he said. Nothing else.

Cassie's body stiffened as he sat next to her. This was so awkward. She didn't know how to begin to explain about the note and everything else. All she knew was that she wanted Micah back. And she wanted him to know it.

Micah cleared his throat. "Cassie, I just want to tell you I'm s—"

Cassie grabbed Micah by the face and kissed him before he could finish.

This was no time for speeches or apologies.

Yes, Cassie knew exactly what she wanted.

And she wasn't afraid to go for it.

PROLOGUE

From: NatalieNYC
To: Aries8
Subject: Summer blues!

Hey Jenna:

Greetings from the Big Apple! How are you?
I'm trying to keep busy now that we don't have a
summer at Lakeview to look forward to. In case you
were wondering exactly how desperate the situation
is, Dad even convinced me to sign up for some improv
classes through a performing arts school here in the
city (there may or may not have been a shopping-
related bribe involved). I know—you can't picture it.
I tried to convince him that acting is *so* not my thing,
but I think he gets excited about me possibly following
in his footsteps. Anyway, maybe now I'll be able to
compare notes with Brynn the next time I see her.
She'll be so excited to have another "thespian" (her
word, of course) among our campmates!

Speaking of . . . do you know what she's doing

this summer, now that Lakeview's shut down? ☹ Have
you heard from anyone else? And what about you, by the
way? Inquiring minds want to know! Tell me I'm not the
only one who is feeling kinda lost without camp.

Write back soon and give me all the gossip!

Miss you,

Nat

From: Aries8
To: NatalieNYC
Subject: Re: Summer blues!

Hiya, city slicker!
    I'm glad to hear that you're keeping busy (but I
would *so* pay money to watch you in an improv class!
LOL! I hope the shopping spree was at least worth it!). I
am, too. My community center has a summer soccer clinic
that I'll go to three times a week, and on the off days, I'll
play tennis with Adam. Naturally, I plan to kick his butt one
hundred percent of the time. We may be twins, but when it
comes to athletic ability, all Blooms are not created equal!
    I got an e-mail from Brynn a few weeks ago, and it
looks like she's planning to do some kind of arts program
in her town. I think she's disappointed; she expected it to
be a huge dose of high-falutin' *theatre*, but when she went
to the orientation, she found out that instead it's some
hippie teacher encouraging her to "engage her body in
creative movement." Like, I think it's mostly interpretive

dance or something. I told her a little interpretive dance never hurt anybody (as far as I know). I'm not sure that she was totally convinced.

Oh, well. I wish we could see each other at Lakeview again, but it looks like that's not in the cards anymore.

At least we've all found *some* way to spend the summer vacation. For better or for worse . . .

Write back soon!

--Jenna

"I love the Film Forum," Natalie sighed, stepping off of the elevator and into the plush hallway of her apartment building. "Where else can you see a movie like *The Wizard of Oz* on the big screen?" She reached into her quilted pink tote bag and fished out a jangly silver key chain, unlocking the door to the Manhattan apartment she shared with her mother.

"Also, they have the best popcorn in the city," her best friend Hannah replied. "What do you think they put in it to make it so extra dee-lish?"

The two girls crossed through the spacious living room and back toward Natalie's pristine bedroom. As usual, her mother was still out, working all hours like the crazed professional that she was. Not that Natalie minded having freedom, unlike some of her friends whose parents were way rule-y.

Rules. Natalie shuddered just thinking about it. Rules probably involved not being allowed to go downtown in a cab with your BFF to watch a movie in an awesome art-house theater.

"Earth to Natalie," Hannah chimed in. "Do you not have an opinion on the great popcorn mystery?"

Natalie shrugged, settling onto her plush bed with her sleek laptop. "As long as it's delicious, why ask questions?"

"Fair enough," Hannah agreed, collapsing next to her on the bed in a heap. "So, does watching an all-time film history classic get you all excited for your improv class?" she continued, propping herself up on one elbow.

Natalie rolled her eyes. "The only place I want to go is Pinkberry after class every week. Seriously—I don't know if I'm cut out to be an actress. That's, like, my dad's thing, or Brynn's." Natalie's father was the movie star Tad Maxwell, who had appeared in a bunch of blockbuster spy movies that were immensely popular. And Brynn was Natalie's friend from summer camp who had a flair for the dramatic.

Natalie could be plenty dramatic herself, when she wanted to. But that didn't mean she had designs on seeing her name in lights. She was happy to leave that to her friends and her father.

"I think it's cute that your dad wants a little mini-me," Hannah insisted. "He's all showing that he cares and stuff. It's sweet."

"Yeah. It's sweet," Natalie said. Then she paused for optimal dramatic effect. "Too bad you can't take those classes for me," Nat countered. She smiled to show she was teasing. Mostly. "Honestly, Han? I never in a million years thought I would say this, but I'm so bummed that Camp Lakeview closed. I really miss it, and all of my camp friends. And you're going to be jetting off to France, so it's going to be super-lonely around here."

"I could stash you in my suitcase; you could stow away," Hannah offered. "We could spend all summer working on our tans on the Riviera!"

Natalie raised an eyebrow. "Are you trying to make me feel worse? You know I have a fear of small, enclosed spaces. So your suitcase—and hence, France—are out.." She sighed. "No France, no Lakeview . . . just a summer of doing breathing exercises and pantomime and stuff . . ." She let her voice trail off as she flipped open her laptop and scanned all her e-mails.

"This from the girl who always claimed to be allergic to nature," Hannah said, shaking her head in disbelief. "I am shocked. Shocked, I tell you."

But Natalie wasn't listening to Hannah anymore; she was too caught up in what she was reading on-screen. Suddenly she sat straight up. "Check out the e-mail that I just got!" She flipped her computer around so that Hannah could see the screen clearly.

"Blah blah Dr. Steve—he's the Lakeview director, right?" Hannah asked, scanning the screen.

Natalie nodded excitedly. "Yep. Well, he was, until Lakeview closed. But keep reading!" She jabbed a pale pink index finger back in the direction of the computer.

"Camp Walla Walla?" Hannah read aloud. "In Connecticut?"

Natalie nearly bounced off the bed and onto the floor, she was so hyped up. She looked at Hannah, her eyes shining with enthusiasm. "Camp Walla Walla," she repeated, "in Connecticut. Dr. Steve is working there this summer!" She paused, giving the information a moment to sink in. "And he wants us to join him!"

"Maybe you got your wish," Hannah said, looking pleased for her friend. "You could be going back to camp after all!"

And for those of you who missed *Camp Confidential*, Books 1–4, catch them all, together in one exciting edition!

camp CONFIDENTIAL

Natalie.
Jenna.
Grace.
Alex.

Four girls.
One thing in common.
Everyone has a secret . . .

Revisit the summer it all began.